Arrowhead in the Black Gumbo

MARY ROBERTSON

ISBN 978-1-954345-10-2 (paperback)
ISBN 978-1-954345-11-9 (digital)

Rushmore Press LLC
1 800 460 9188
www.rushmorepress.com

Printed in the United States of America

Prologue

In Texas, there is a deep, black dirt that holds water well but crusts over in the Texas sun. It is unique because it is a combination of organic material, sand, and clay. This is black gumbo.

The two dug quickly as they could with rock, sticks, and hands. The deep, black earth was hard to turn up in the dry time, but it had to be done. They would never forget this spot, their tree. It only seemed fitting that they put their precious possessions here to come get later.

Little did the brokenhearted lovers know, later would not come for them. It would be generations for them to be united in this time. It would take a daughter returning home.

Chapter 1

Evelyn looked up into the sky through the leaves of the oak tree. She inhaled deeply. It was hot, but the shade offered some comfort. She was in her favorite spot. The old oak tree had a branch that lay out from the trunk at a ninety-degree angle, as if it were made that way just for her. From the time she was a little girl, she would run to climb this tree and lie on her branch to stare up at the sky. As she grew older, this spot became her thinking place, her quiet spot where she stole away, just to contemplate life. But right now, she was just taking a break from a hot, summer workday. There was always a lot to do on the old hundred-acre farm.

"Evey!" cried an older man. His blue eyes showed from under his dirty old cowboy hat. "Time to get back at it, sister."

Her grandfather was a short man with the happiest of laugh lines on his face, a button nose, and a full head of salt-and-pepper hair. Evey was his pet name for Evelyn. She lived with her grandparents on their farm and was grateful to be with them, even if she had to help around the farm with chores. She wouldn't have it any other way though. Evey enjoyed working with her hands mending fences and working the land with her grandfather.

"Coming, Grandpa!" she hollered.

Evey knew he would know where she was at. Her grandparents always knew she would be in her tree when she had a moment to herself.

She climbed down the tree gingerly and landed with a thud. She hurriedly put her socks and boots back on. She couldn't climb with shoes on. She laughed when she thought about her grandpa telling her she had monkey toes. She jogged over to the gate and opened it, careful to latch it well behind her. She didn't want to let the cows in again and have them get into her grandma's herb garden. She laughed thinking about her short, round grandma with her gray bun running out of the house with a broom to shoo the cows out of her herbs. Although her grandma was small, she was fierce, and shame on anyone who got on her bad side—including a two-thousand-pound cow!

Evelyn got through the gate and met her grandpa's smile. He had a way of reading her mind.

"It was funny wasn't it, sister? I just hope to never make Grandma mad enough at me to chase me with a broom!"

They both burst out in laughter. He put his arm around her shoulder, and they were off to go work up the hayfield. They needed to finish breaking the ground to get it ready. Their rusty old, orange Allis Chambers tractor complained with the disk, an implement that in fact has many small metal discs to till the soil, as it dug into the deep dirt—the black gumbo, as they called it.

Evelyn loved the smell of dirt—a rich, wet, earthy smell that made her feel so small in comparison to all around her. She loved the potential it held. And although it was hard to grow stuff in this dirt, when it did grow, it yielded so well. She bent down to pick up a handful of dirt and rub it between her fingers. It was perfect. The top would get hard and crust over, but that hard layer would keep the moisture underneath to help the roots of whatever was planted.

But today, it was for the cows. They had to get the hayfield taken care of so it would start producing enough over the winter to store up for the droughts of summer. With fall and winter approaching, the rain would come—time to work the land and prepare it to host vegetation. Grandpa busted up the ground in their little hay meadow, and Evey went behind pulling up unsavory vegetation. Then Evey went to spread fertilizer.

Grandma said the news forecasted rain for the weekend, but her knees were saying it would be more like tomorrow. Grandma was always full of wisdom and had said, "I guess you take the good with the bad getting older. Stuff hurts more, but you're a walking weather forecast." Grandpa always said Grandma just knew things. But it was stuff that was passed down from generations of family—things that can't be learned in a workbook.

After they had finished up, Evey and her grandpa looked at their little patch and were pleased. They always stood side by side, she a little taller than he.

He patted her back and said, "I'm going to walk over to the pen to check the new calf and then head on up to the house to clean up."

They had a first-time momma cow with a new baby. The cow had a hard time birthing her first calf, and they had had to pull the calf to save them both. Pulling a calf is messy business, but Evey would do anything it took to give something a fighting a chance and loved anything that was a baby. The calf was the cutest brown-and-white doe-eyed thing. In fact, Evey had named her Doe. The cow and calf were doing fine, but they kept them in the pen to keep an eye on them to be sure.

"Okeydokey. I'll head that way soon. I just want to check the gate on the edge of the meadow. I may have tapped it with the fertilizer bin," she said as she nodded and made a slight wince. "But I'll fix it if I messed it up."

"I know you will. You're a good girl and a hard worker. I saw you bump it, but I was going to keep it to myself." He winked as he smiled, turning to walk to the pin.

Evelyn was tired, and her big feet felt heavy, so she shucked off her boots and socks. She loved the feel of the ground beneath her bare feet. She laughed again, thinking about Grandpa telling her she must have been part of the Blackfoot tribe because her feet were always dirty. In reality, they were called the Blackfoot tribe because of the color of the moccasins they wore and didn't go barefoot at all. But she never corrected him and just laughed. Evey was a history buff and loved to learn all she could.

She looked up from taking off her boots and came back to reality. There was something to do. She just had to check the gate before she went in to wash and have supper. She hoped her grandma was making fried chicken, mashed potatoes, gravy, and maybe some summer squash. Her mouth was watering by the time she made it to the gate.

She pushed on the big, round fence post. It didn't move. It looked a little crooked, but during the hot summer months, things tended to move a little with the cracking of the ground. She walked over to the other post. That wasn't the one she clipped, but she would check it all the same.

She put her hand on top and wiggled. It moved slightly. She looked down at the ground to see if there was a visible gap. She might need to tamp it or add some quick-setting cement the next day to secure it. She looked down to study it. No visible gap, but at the top of the dirt right next to the post, she saw something.

Chapter 2

$\mathcal{E}$velyn stared down for a moment. At first it looked like just a piece of brown rock. As she bent down to study it further, she saw that it was in fact a rock, but it looked weathered. Rocks on the surface of the dirt of course got weathered, but one under the earth would not be as much so. It would have been protected from outer elements.

She got down on her knees and stooped her head low for a closer look. It wouldn't make sense for a rock in the ground to be so weathered and one side flat. She could see just its edge, so she gripped it with two fingers and worked it back and forth until it came loose. She pulled it up. It was an arrowhead! She was shocked and excited to find an arrowhead in the black gumbo.

Her grandma had told her stories of Indians who had lived on this land but moved, leaving her great-great-great—maybe one or two more *great*s—grandma to live in peace. Evey wasn't really sure of the whole story. Native peoples didn't just leave their land. Evey always assumed they must have had a good reason. Grandma told the story that had been passed down, and it had been passed down so many generations that Evey just knew there had to be more to it. Evey loved rocks and history, and this was just over the top. She placed the arrowhead in the palm of hand. The rock felt so cold and then felt as if it had a heartbeat of its own.

As she looked down, her hand was not her own. She was looking at a boy's hand—a sun-kissed brown hand!

The hand was working on the arrowhead with another rock to make the edges come out smooth and sharp. She seemed to be at a stream. She could hear the water and the wind in the trees. It looked like the stream on the back side of the property but different. The trees were smaller. She knew the place. She looked down at the arrowhead in her hand and felt something—a feeling she didn't know how to describe, as if she knew something but didn't know what it was.

She dropped the arrowhead as if it were a thousand degrees to the touch. She was still at the gate along the freshly busted-up black dirt.

Evelyn eyed the arrowhead, scared and intrigued. Dare she pick it up again? She reached down slower than a sloth. She carefully picked it up with two fingers. Nothing. She slowly sat it on edge in her hand and then let it fall even slower, flat onto her palm. She was back at the water's edge.

She wanted to see whose eyes she was looking through. She peered into the water to try to catch a reflection. The first thing she saw were deep brown eyes that seemed to be looking into her soul. They were intense, as if they could see everything. Long, brown hair fell to the shoulders of a young boy, about eight or nine maybe. He was working diligently on this arrowhead to make it just right. He had a single feather braided in his hair behind his right ear. Evey touched her right ear to see the hand move up. Strong hands, she noticed, and she caressed the strong jawline and highbrow. The lips were a thin line of deep pink. Everything seemed strong about this boy—a hunter in the making, maybe.

Evey was admiring this ancient person and thinking how astonishingly handsome this weird, dark-eyed, long-haired boy was. There seemed to be something lost in her own time. Then she heard shouts and screams, and then she looked up toward the trees and felt scared, and a language she didn't know was being shouted, and she felt like life itself may end.

Evelyn threw the arrowhead out onto the ground. She eyed it conspicuously and tried to calm her heart that was beating frantically. She couldn't leave it there, but she really didn't want to touch it again. Evey looked at it a long while—she had to take it in. She carefully picked it up with two fingers and placed it in her pocket and headed up the little narrow road, with her dirty boots and worn socks, to the old farmhouse. She must have looked disheveled when she came in.

"I was about to send Tudley to find you and tell you to come on supper is almost ready and"—her grandma looked at her—"are you okay, honey?"

Evey carefully pulled the arrowhead from her pocket with two fingers.

"Oh my goodness! How neat! Baby, come look what Evey found!"

She heard Grandpa grunt as he got up from his favorite brown chair in the living room.

"Lookey there, sister! That is what you kids would call cool! But don't go telling anyone about it. We don't want the museum nerds coming and digging up our whole place hoping to find something else," he said.

"Don't worry. I won't," Evelyn said with such conviction that her grandparents looked from one another curiously.

Evelyn held the arrowhead out toward her grandma who put her hand out. Evey sat it in her grandma's palm and watched her closely. Nothing.

"Are you okay, honey?" she asked again.

"Yes. I guess I'm just worn out. I'm going to clean up for supper," Evey said.

Grandma nodded, eyeing her suspiciously, placing the arrowhead in a very old, blue medicine jar on the bar.

Grandma loved all things old and collected old jars—medicine jars, in particular. Grandma's herb garden was for more than seasonings for chicken. She grew herbs to make natural remedies for all sorts of ailments. Evey always lovingly called her, her own personal witch doctor.

She smiled a little as she turned to make the short trek to the bathroom and felt her head to wonder if she was indeed suffering from heat exhaustion.

Chapter 3

In the shower, Evelyn kept seeing the Indian boy in her mind. She wondered who he was and what had happened, and she remembered the fear she felt as she heard the frantic yell in a language she couldn't understand. She shivered in the shower, even though she had piping-hot water rushing over her tall, slender fit body. She washed and watched the dirt swirl down the drain and wondered if she were in fact crazy. Who would believe her if and when she said anything? They would surely blame it on the heat. She rinsed her long, auburn hair and turned the water off.

She grabbed her towel and blotted her face, and as she closed her golden brown eyes, she saw the deep, dark brown eyes staring into hers.

"Who are you?" she wondered aloud, and Tudley barked as if to answer.

Tudley was kind of her dog. Evey found the little coyote pup abandoned and alone four years ago. She bottle-fed him, and he stayed by her side when she was home.

"I guess you would believe me, Tudley. After all, you're a wild animal who runs with a teenage girl," she said, smiling at her coyote, beaming with pride.

Evey took a look in the mirror. All that work in the summer sun had her freckles darkened up and more spotting along her forehead. Her nose seemed a little sunburnt, but all in all, it was okay. She checked her fingernails to make sure she got all the dirt out from under them. Grandma would get her if she didn't. She smiled.

Her grandparents were amazing. They took her in when she was eight because her parents were killed in a tragic car accident. Thank God she was at a friend's house when it happened. She remembered being excited when her grandparents' old, blue single-cab Chevy pulled up to get her. Evelyn had thought it was such a great surprise.

As they got closer, she could tell they had both been crying. They smiled at her, got her bags, and thanked her friend's parents and put her in the middle of the truck seat and pulled out of the driveway. Her grandpa was driving and had his arm around her shoulders and holding onto her grandma's shoulder with his weathered hand, and her grandma had her hand on her little bony knee.

They both squeezed her and said, "We are taking you back home with us, baby doll."

There was something so definite and final in their voices, and she knew that wasn't a normal sleepover.

Evey teared up as she thought about the funeral. Her grandparents were as perfect as they could be through it all and made Evey feel at home. It wasn't too hard to be at home there because it was her home away from home, and she loved it there. Evey had spent weeks there during the summers before her parents died. It was just as much home as with her parents.

She spent many hours in her tree, crying alone. Her grandma would watch her through the kitchen window over the sink.

"It's okay to need some time alone," she would tell her. "But don't forget who is back in here ready to love on you. You can always tell me anything and never feel bad for how you are feeling."

She never made her feel bad about how she felt, and Evey loved her so much for that.

Her grandma taught her all about herbs and their medicinal uses, like her mother before had taught her and the one before and the one before. The women of Evey's family had always been known as great healers. They weren't doctors, though—just really good mothers who knew how to use the plants around them. Her great-great-grandmother could remove warts by rubbing them and saying something, and her grandmother was an impeccable judge of character and could save you some heartache if you'd just listen to her. Grandpa always said, "I've learned to just believe whatever it is your grandma says. It makes life easier." Maybe Grandma would do the same with her.

Evelyn went to the dinner table. It was an old table with yellow chairs and a bench seat by a window outlooking grandma's herb garden. The window seat was her favorite. Her grandma did make fried chicken. There is nothing like chicken fried in a cast-iron skillet. She was eating and made the decision to tell her grandparents about what happened. Evey felt like she would explode if she didn't tell someone besides Tudley.

"I know this sounds crazy, but I have to tell you something," Evey started.

She went through the whole story and told them about the stream and the Indian boy and how scared she felt. She felt her face turn red and knew her feelings must have shown. How could they not think she was crazy? They looked at her, relieved. Evey was confused.

"You don't think I'm crazy?" she asked.

They laughed.

"We thought something bad happened with Danny," Grandma said.

Danny was the boy from down the road she had been dating since freshman year, and they were still going strong now into their senior year. He was a tall, blue-eyed, blond-haired boy with dimples and a sweet, sheepish smile. He was the only boy she ever dated, and her grandparents were having a hard time with their granddaughter dating—Grandma especially.

She loved Danny, and she had seen him grow up. But something there wasn't clear for her. As in Grandma's way, she didn't say anything because some life lessons are better learned by living them. But they trusted their honest granddaughter and they had watched the young boy grow up.

He was from a wealthy old family, the Baileys, and anyone would be happy to marry into them. His family had been a prominent name for as long as their little town was there. Danny's mother was a very arrogant woman who thought no one was good enough for her son. She didn't hide her apprehension about her son being with Evey, the dirty farmer girl. It was so hard for her grandparents to go through the dating stage again. They had only ever been through this one other time—with Evey's mom—and Evey's was harder. Kids were so much more different now.

"But seriously, y'all. I picked up an arrowhead and saw and felt things," she insisted.

Grandma looked at her and took a deep breath.

"Honey, we all have gifts. My mother had dreams and knew when someone going to die. I just sense things, and your mother could get rid of the warts too. You can pass it down every other generation, and she was who got picked. It kills me that gift died with her," Grandma trailed off.

Grandpa took over for her. He always knew when to step in for his wife.

"The women in this family are all special, Evey, and why would you be any different? It takes a smart, strong man to marry a woman of this family. The men weren't always smart, but the last few of us were." He winked at her.

"So this is a gift?" Evey asked, confused. "I pick up an ancient arrowhead and see something and that's a gift?"

"I should say it's better than dreams and knowing when someone is going to die," said Grandma.

"Is something wrong with us?" she questioned, grabbing her Grandma's hand.

"No, honey. We are normal. My momma always thought it was because we live here and have ties to this land. You know the Indians ran this land for a very long time before we came about. I've only been told stories, so keep in mind that we might not know the whole truth and we don't ever want to be arrogant and assume anything about the Indians. We were close with the Indians at one time, and they taught Sarah, the first one of us here, the treasures of the plants and herbs around us for medicine. But then they were gone, and it was just our family matriarch and patriarch. You'll be just fine." Grandma smiled.

"But everything is okay with Danny?" Grandpa broke the tension, and Evey burst out laughing.

"Oh my gosh, Grandpa! Yes. Nothing has happened there!" Evey shrieked out.

Evelyn sat across her grandparents with a full belly and just admired them. They loved each other so much and her. She thought it was quite possible she adored them as much as they her. She couldn't help but smile. They didn't condemn her, or call her crazy, or push her to do anything else. They just let her sit there and take it in. Her grandma looked at her and smiled back contagiously.

"What are you thinking about, my honey?" she asked.

"I'm thinking how lucky I am to have the two of you and hope to have a marriage as solid as yours one day. I've seen you laugh, cry, be angry, and go through the worst thing possible and still be standing together and love me through my despair. I want a love like yours—lasting and strong. I am strong because of your love."

Evelyn felt whole for a moment in their presence.

"You know, you saved us as much as we saved you, sister. Having you is what kept us going. And I don't care what you see or what your gifts are. You are my baby girl. Don't fret. And I'll still break Danny's legs if he breaks your heart," Grandpa said, pounding his chest like an ape.

They all laughed, and Grandma nodded in approval of Grandpa's threat and manly chest thump.

Evelyn's eyes glanced to the top of the bar to the little, blue medicine jar and its contents. Her curiosity was running wild, and she still saw the dark brown eyes when she closed her golden brown beauties. But now she needed rest. Her body ached and was tired from the day's labor.

Chapter 4

Tudley followed Evelyn to bed. He always slept at the foot of her bed, almost on her feet. He was the best guard dog. He was very possessive of his queen. There's a special bond between human and animal when you bottle-feed them. She pulled the old patchwork quilt up to her ear and tried to fall into the bliss of sleep. She was just on the edge of that blissfulness when the owls started talking outside her window. She got up and took the two steps to her window that overlooked an old magnolia tree. In the springtime, its blossoms would fill the house with its sweet, fragrant smell. She loved that, but right now, it was acting as a perch to two little barn owls.

Oh no, she thought.

"What are you doing here?" she asked them as she cracked the window open.

Her family passed down old wives' tales; one of which was that when you hear owls talking, someone is going to die and death comes in threes.

"Who's it going to be then and why did you come to tell me?"

It seemed a burden looming over her of someone's impending death. She closed the window back, and Tudley looked up at her, ears twitching to and fro. She couldn't sleep now.

Evey went to the kitchen to get a drink of water. She turned the faucet on and inhaled deeply. She would drink straight from the faucet. The well water there was wonderful, not a shallow well or a well that stunk with the methane that can get trapped in the well. It was delicious and crisp. She took two big gulps, and her eyes once again went to the blue medicine jar.

She took two graceful long steps with her long legs to the bar and reached up and grabbed the jar and just stared in for what seemed like a long time. She felt the need to know more. Her curiosity won out.

She reached in with two fingers and gently plucked the arrowhead up and out of the jar. Evey had noticed that as long as it wasn't flat in her palm, she was okay. She held it with her thumb and pointer in front of her face. She eyed it dubiously and took a deep breath.

Maybe I should sit at the table, Evey pondered.

She did in fact sit down. She wasn't sure what she would see. Evey laid the brown rock flat in her palm. The arrowhead went hot and felt heavy.

The alien language was being screamed. She smelled smoke. There was a fire. She looked down at her hand to see the brown hand again. A scary-looking man with nothing but hide pants came running out of the wood and was yelling.

"I don't understand," she tried to holler, but he acted like he couldn't hear her.

The boy nodded, and she felt her head nod too.

Okay, so I couldn't understand, but this boy could, Evey concluded.

He hurried and grabbed a leather-looking thing on the ground and filled it up with water from the stream as quickly as he could.

Evey tried to see his reflection. He looked worried but stoic—a look she knew. Her grandpa had it for her so often.

He filled his container of sorts up and ran after the scary-looking guy with some sort of piercing through his lip. When she came out of the woods, they were in a clearing. It looked so familiar but younger. The trees weren't as tall as she knew them to be now and there was no farmhouse. There was a little wood cabin there, and it was on fire! She felt sick.

A large muscular man with a leather necklace and feathers in his hair was running toward her—or should she say *him*? She was seeing through this Indian boy's eyes right now. The man was running toward him holding something. Then she saw—it was a young girl. She was covered in ash and was unconscious.

"Oh my god. What happened?" Evey was holding her breath.

She—he—ran to the big man and pulled the water out.

This boy's brown hands cradled the head of a young girl with strawberry blonde hair and gently poured water into her mouth, and the big Indian blew over her face. After a moment, she sputtered and gasped for air. Then her golden brown eyes popped open.

Evey was abruptly interrupted by the owls again. She dropped the arrowhead on the table as if it had sliced right through her hand. Had they followed her to the kitchen?

"I really don't want to know when or who is going to die guys," she said scornfully at the owls who were now perched on the old lamp outside the chicken coop.

The tiredness hit Evey in a wave, and she fell asleep head on the table and dreamt of burning girls and Indian boys.

Chapter 5

$\mathcal{E}$velyn woke in the morning to her Grandma gently rubbing her shoulder.

"My heavens, honey. What on earth are you doing here?" Grandma said, looking worried.

"The owls were talking last night, and I couldn't sleep, so I came to get a drink of water and . . ." she trailed off, looking down at the table.

Grandma saw the arrowhead and nodded with understanding.

"I just wanted to know who the boy was, and now all I have are more questions. I know the land is ours, but it's so different, and there's a young girl. I know, I know her. And then, the owls followed me here and were being loud, and I dropped the arrowhead, and next thing I know, you're waking me."

The words just flooded from Evey.

Grandma looked uneasy.

"The owls followed you, you said?"

"I guess so. They were in the magnolia tree and then the lamp by the coop. I feel like they are trying to tell me something, but I really don't want the death too," Evey said, shuddering.

Grandma went about making coffee and two eggs just like Evey liked them—not fried all the way, hard and not runny, and like jelly in the middle. Toast and eggs were her breakfast of choice, and she had always been a coffee drinker from the time she was big enough to ask for coffee. Grandpa would tell her it would put hair on her chest, which made her giggle to herself.

"Is Danny coming to get you today?" Grandma asked.

Evey looked up, shocked. Her mind had been on Indians and fires, she forgot about their date tonight. One of his cousins were getting married.

"Yes he is. And I better figure out what to wear. I have to look decent to go be with all his family," she said.

Grandma looked up over her coffee and said, "You'd look good in a feed sack!"

Evelyn was glad it was Saturday and her and Grandpa got all the major work done yesterday. Today was just the normal chores of feeding chickens and checking on all the animals. She still needed to figure out what to wear, but she had time. She would rather take a minute to go check on the new calf.

She walked slowly down the little dirt road, looking around to see if she could imagine this place before—before the road she was walking, before the cow pens, before the house, or before the hay meadow or the windmill. Her mind kept wandering back to the time she had seen and the little boy who so gently gave water to a young girl in trouble. She had so many questions but was brought out of her daze when she heard a rattling.

The rattling sounded angry. She knew what lay in front of her without looking. That was the sound of death.

Were those dang owls foretelling my death? Evey thought. *I sure hope not.*

In these situations, you don't have time to think—you just act. She peered down to see a long, very big rattlesnake coiled right in the middle of the pathway. Snakes can strike a long distance, and she eyed it quickly to try to see how far she thought it might reach.

In the split second it took her to analyze the situation, she threw her water bottle she always carried in the heat at the snake. The nasty thing struck at the bottle, and she ran for the house. She made it to the shed in a few minutes. Grandpa had spied her running down the road, and he was moving toward her as fast as his short legs could.

"What is it, sister?" he hollered.

"Snake. In path. Big rattler" was all Evey could manage out through gasping for air.

Grandpa grabbed his long shovel and was headed down the path.

Evey hurried after her grandpa after she caught her breath.

No one should take on a rattler on their own, just in case, Evey told herself. *Oh no, Grandpa . . . the owls.*

By the time she made it back, Grandpa had a dead snake over the end of his shovel. Snakes gave her the creeps, but she also felt sad at the loss of life, anytime there was. But she would rather see the snake go than one of them.

Grandpa tossed the rattler from the large snake at her and said, "Yours."

For some reason, her family always kept at least the rattler off the snake. Her grandma said that if you receive rattles from someone, no harm will come to you while that person is around or that it may be a good-luck charm if you keep it after killing one. Evey preferred to think the first and believed no harm would come to her with her grandpa around. Although she spotted it and he killed it, there may be room for discrepancy.

Many times her grandpa would stretch the hides out on a board and keep them. Today she needed a little luck.

What in the heck am I going to wear to that wedding? Evey introspected.

Without realizing it, she was rubbing the rattle.

"Dang wives' tales!" Evey sighed as she turned to head to the house.

Chapter 6

Evelyn eyed her closet while sitting on her bed. Her Sunday best was hung neatly. She had several dresses. She attended church regularly with her grandparents. She wasn't very good at dressing up. She preferred casual dress like jeans or shorts and a T-shirt and, if she had the choice, no shoes. Tonight, she would have to wear heels.

Beauty is pain, she thought.

She wanted to look classy with Danny's family. They were an old well-to-do family who had been in the area as long as hers. It just seemed natural that the two of them would be an item. They were a handsome couple together. It seemed as if Danny's mother didn't care for Evey or her family, but Evey had no clue why.

Oh well. We don't pick 'em, Evey concluded.

Her eyes finally settled on a knee-length, light turquoise-colored dress. It was one of her favorites, and she didn't think she had worn it around them. It had short sleeves with a small, rectangular section of white crystals at the top. The dress was form fitting but with ruffles, so it didn't seem too risqué.

She looked fabulous in it. Her auburn hair and golden eyes were highlighted by the dress color. She wore a single strand of pearls and pearl studs that were her mother's. Evey wondered what she would do with her wild long hair. It would get frizzy and wild at the drop of a hat.

"Grandma!" she shouted towards the kitchen from her room.

Her grandma was in her doorway in a minute.

"What do you need, honey?" she said, smiling, looking at her granddaughter.

"I don't know what to do with my hair." She frowned, looking into the mirror on her dresser.

"Let's see," said grandma, walking over to her. "Sit down and hand me your bobby pins."

Grandma bossed her.

Evey obeyed, knowing she needed the help. A ponytail and a braid were about the only two things she knew how to do. Grandma loved doing her hair. It reminded her of her daughter. She started braiding a piece back and pinned something there and used her fingers to make ringlets in front of her ears and bam—a beautiful updo.

"I always told your mom that I wished my hair was like hers. You have her hair, as wild as the wind but so beautiful," Grandma said, looking into the mirror with her hands on Evey's shoulders.

"Thank you. I love you," Evelyn told her grandma, grabbing her hands and squeezing tight, staring deeply into her eyes.

Her hair was in fact gorgeous. It was braided back at the side and put up in a cascading fountain of wild curls but still beautiful. Evelyn put on some mascara and a light pink lip gloss, spritzed on some perfume, and looked in the mirror one more time. She was a "less is more" type with makeup. Rightfully so because she was most beautiful in her natural state. She was ready and looked so pretty. She hoped Danny would stop in his tracks. Every girl just wants to hear she's beautiful.

There was a knock at the door, and she heard Grandpa get it.

"Sister, some strange boy is here looking for you!" she heard the jubilee in her grandpa's voice.

She smiled and went out to make her entrance. Danny was in the kitchen. That's just where everyone convened. She was walking carefully as not to fall in the nude two-strap heels she had on. She was looking down as she crossed the threshold into the kitchen and looked up to see Danny. He was smiling at her.

"You look so beautiful, Evelyn," he said with a proud smile.

"You don't look so bad yourself sir," she said back.

In fact, he looked quite dashing. He had on starched blue jeans with his dress boots, a white pearl snap, a navy blue sports coat, and, of course, his silver felt cowboy hat.

"I feel like I should be putting some flowers on your wrist or something," Danny said with his sheepish smile.

"Well, Danny, flowers are never a bad idea," Grandma said, winking at him.

"Y'all best get going or you're going to be late to the wedding. Grandma and I have a hot date," Grandpa said in turn, winking at Danny.

"Oh, Grandpa!" said Evey.

She hugged both of her grandparents, Danny hugged Grandma and shook Grandpa's hand, and the two young lovebirds headed out.

Danny was a gentleman. He opened the truck door of his new Chevy Silverado for Evelyn and shut the door gently and ran around and got in.

"I've been looking forward to this all week," he said, grabbing her hand and putting it to his mouth to kiss it.

"Me too! I've worked my tail off so I wouldn't have to really do anything today," she replied.

Danny's family was rice farmers, so Danny worked just as hard as she did with his family. But the Baileys were well off, hence his new truck.

He drove down the mile-long dirt road to get out of the farm and stopped at the very end of the road before getting onto the county road to head to the church for the wedding.

"What are you doing?" Evey asked, one brow raised.

Danny put it in park and pulled Evelyn to him and kissed her. He kissed her thoroughly and finished up with a few little smacks on her lips. She felt her face grow hot and knew she was blushing. She was out of breath.

"I couldn't wait any longer to do that. You're so damn beautiful. I'll have the most beautiful girl on my arm," Danny said. "Just don't tell my cousin that!"

She busted out laughing and kissed him on the cheek.

"Well, I know I'll have the best-looking cowboy to hold on to." She winked at him, and they both laughed.

He put it back in Drive and held her hand as they made their way to the little, white church.

They held hands the whole way to the church. They were still a sweet young couple. They had grown up together and experienced many firsts together—first day of school, first T-ball game, first kiss—but there was still one first they had not yet done. They both went to church, so maybe it was conviction; mostly, Evey was scared and unsure, but man did she want him badly at times. Right now was one of those times.

He hopped off the truck to come around and let her out, and he leaned in to kiss her one more time before they had to walk in and no longer be alone.

When he leaned in, she turned toward him, spreading her legs to let him step in. He was so close to her, she could feel the bulge in his jeans on her more intimate areas. She had tightened her legs around his hips and kissed him harder and held his neck to not let him go.

He pulled just barely up from her with his nose still touching hers and sighed deeply, "I wish I could just stay her forever with you, but the wedding is about to start, and we certainly don't want anyone to come looking for us, especially while we look like this!"

He laughed and she did too. She let her grip with her legs go, and he stepped aside and adjusted himself and held his hand out to her to help her out. She brushed her dress down and looked up at the handsome blue-eyed guy and smiled. He stooped and kissed her cheek, and off they went into the church.

Chapter 7

It was a really nice wedding. There were white roses with hints of pink, and it was very elegant. Evelyn had sighed sweetly with the reading of their vows and couldn't help but smile with the way the groom looked at his bride. She guessed she must have squeezed Danny's hand because he pulled her hand closer to him.

His parents always kept an eye on the two. They were always wanting to see how they acted together. They didn't have anything against Evelyn but always had an air about them. They were the country-club type of folks, and they expected their son to marry the same, and Evey was more of a down-home type.

The reception was in an elaborate hall that must have cost a fortune. There were lights strung about everywhere, and the floral arrangements on the table were breathtaking. Evelyn and Danny sat together and had normal conversation with the family at the assigned dinner table. They got the usual "You two have been together forever" and "Well, what's your plans after graduation?" They endured the conversation, and it was helped when a filet mignon was served.

Pricy indeed, she thought.

The Baileys were always trying to impress the general public.

They finished eating, and the dance floor was ready. She was so relieved when Danny asked her to dance. They loved to dance and moved well together. They made it through the first song and were smiling at each other.

"Are you okay, babe?" he asked.

She frowned and said, "My feet are killing me!"

"Then take your shoes off," he said matter-of-factly.

"No, I can't take my shoes off in front of your family!" she said in a hot whisper.

He eyed her intently. "Fine then."

He picked her right up and whisked her off the dance floor with everyone staring, mouths wide open.

"Danny!" she squealed.

He laughed and hauled her off outside to a bench and sat her down and pulled her legs into his lap and gently pulled her heels off and started to rub her feet.

"Ooh," she moaned. "That's nice."

He looked up and gave her a mischievous grin.

"You like it, huh? What if . . ." he trailed off, massaging higher.

Evey looked at him between slit eyelids.

"Do you want to get out of here?" he asked.

"Don't we need to tell everyone bye?" she replied with a question.

"So you do want to leave then?" he said, smiling.

She just smiled back.

He jumped up and said, "Well, let's go say bye then."

They made their rounds telling everyone goodbye and wishing the newlyweds well and left.

In the truck, he asked her, "Where do you want to go? I don't have to get you home just yet."

He is so cute, Evey thought.

She smiled at him and said not a word.

At the next stoplight, he said, "Well . . ."

Evelyn scooted closer to him, kissed his neck, and took his hand and placed it in between her thighs. Danny looked at her, surprised but definitely happy about the current circumstance. He bent his head to her and kissed her and let his hand wander the rest of the way and, to his shock, found there was nothing there to impede his progress.

He was slow and gentle, and Evelyn opened her legs and pushed herself toward him, and she let out a moan when he caressed her. He kissed her again and took her hand to his stiff member through his pants.

Honk! Honk! Honk!

They had completely forgotten they were at a light!

"Shit," Danny said, laughing and went on.

They went down an old dirt backcountry road. Evelyn knew where they were going. Danny's family had an old camp house they would let guests stay in. She was ready. She was nervous. But everything in her body was pulsating for him, and she didn't want to stop.

He pulled into the bumpy long drive, still holding on to her. He barely got it in park when she straddled him and thrust her tongue into his mouth, steering wheel in her back not bothering her a bit. She could feel he was excited for her too. He held her tight and kissed her back hard and bit her bottom lip. She finally came up for breath and looked at him.

"Can I take you in?" Danny asked.

She nodded.

He opened the door and swung them both around, never moving her from his lap, and carried her in. Her long legs wrapped around his waist, and she was pushing herself hard against him, wanting to feel him. They continued to kiss as he carried her to the camp house.

Danny got the door open and fumbled for the light switch. It was hard to find with Evey clinging to him, but he found it and made his way to the bed. He wanted her so badly, he throbbed. He gently laid her on the bed and just looked at her.

"Danny," she said. "Unzip my dress."

She stood up and turned her back to him. He slowly unzipped it and let it fall to the ground. He looked at her back and her bare rump and took a deep breath. He then lightly touched her as he moved his hands up to unclasp her bra. She had goose bumps rise all over, and he noticed and smiled. Then he moved his hands up her spine to her head where he pulled bobby pins one by one out of her hair. She turned to face him, and he took a deep breath in. She was flawless. Her long, curly hair cascading down to her breasts, her perky round breasts—he needed to touch her.

"My turn," she said and she began to pop his pearl snaps one by one. "Oh to heck with it!"

Evey just started ripping Danny's shirt open.

His body was chiseled. His pecs were hard and nipples were standing, and so was something else still stuck in his jeans. She slowly moved her hands down to his belt and unfastened it and worked on the button and his zipper and then, sliding both hands in his waistband, pushed his pants down. She looked at him. He was handsome and ready for her.

Danny pulled her to him so their naked bodies could touch for the first time. He was hard and warm. He had his hands around her face and neck and was pulling her up to meet his lips. They kissed, and he moved his kiss down her neck and grasped her breasts, and she sighed. He picked her up in one motion and laid her on the bed, and he lay on top of her, kissing and touching, and she in turn did the same.

Danny stopped.

"Do you want—"

Evelyn cut him off with a kiss and opened her legs more to him and pushed herself toward him. He got the picture. Slowly he put himself inside her. She gasped.

"Are you okay?" he asked, looking worried.

"Yes," she breathed out. "Just go slow, okay?"

He nodded and kissed her more slowly and began to move slowly inside her.

It hurt but wasn't unbearable. She found the rhythm of it and wanted more, pulling him tightly to her.

"A little faster," she said.

He looked surprised and amused. He moved a little faster, thrusting a little harder. She moaned. He moaned, and in an instant, they lay in a crumpled heap on the bed, breathing hard.

Evelyn was giggling, and Danny was feeling pretty good with himself. He kissed her on the cheek and jumped up.

"Where are you going?" Evelyn asked.

"To get us a drink. I need some water," he said, smiling.

He didn't bother putting clothes back on; she smiled as she saw his backside go out of the room. She got up and put his shirt on and just pulled it closed like a robe. She decided to explore as there were a bunch of antiques in the old camp house.

Chapter 8

Evelyn was walking around only in Danny's shirt and smiling as she relived every moment that had just happened. She made her way over to an old armoire and opened it up. Inside was an even older wooden box that looked like it had been through every war ever fought. She opened it up and peered in.

There were odd pieces and bits inside. She saw some old coins and brooches, and at the very bottom, she saw an old chain that looked like brass. She pulled at it, and up came an extremely old pocket watch. It was dinged a little and had initials crudely carved into it, "DVB."

She eyed it, wondering how old it actually was and whose it was. She placed it in her palm to open it, and as she did, she felt the familiar odd sensation of the piece itself having its own heartbeat, and once again her vision was not her own.

She smelled fire. She looked down at her hands to see an older white man's hands with dirty fingernails. He seemed to have on a nice coat. She looked around to notice she was in a small one-room cabin. It was really old. It had a dirt floor.

On the bed she saw a woman who looked really sick. She couldn't get out of bed. She was just saying, "Please, please," in a hushed, terrified voice.

Evey wanted to run to her to help, but the body she was in stood still.

"No way in hell. We can let anyone outta here," bellowed the man.

She heard a baby cry and a cough and gasp.

Oh no, there was a sick baby too, Evey thought.

A back door swung open, and a man came staggering in with a water jug.

"What are you doing in my house?" the man asked, terror in his eyes.

Her body spoke in a weird English accent, "We heard your family had taken ill. You can't be spreading your sickness to all the townsfolk, eh?"

"Oh god, no," pleaded the man. "I promise we won't leave the house, sir."

"You wife is already as good as dead. Look at her, man. And the babe sounds not far off," the body Evey possessed snarled back.

She would never say anything like that. Her stomach felt sick. Her hand reached for something—a stick with a flame at the end.

The other man ran forward at him.

"*No*! You would murder my wife and child?"

"Sometimes the loss of a few is better than the loss of many," said the old man with dirty fingernails.

Evey felt nauseas. It wasn't her, but her body was not her own in the moment.

And he threw the lit stick on a pile of dirty bedclothes. Instantly they went up in flames. The other man cried out in terror and tried to put it out, but the body Evey was in kicked him down; and the man doubled over and wheezed.

The flames went to the bed, and the woman let out the most awful shriek Evey had ever heard. Before the flames overcame her, Evey noticed her fiery golden brown eyes locked with hers. She stared at the man who took her life, and he ran out like a coward and barred the door shut.

"Good riddance to you and your illness," he said aloud.

Another scream—a younger more faint scream—rang out.

The baby!

Evelyn threw the pocket watch. She was shaking all over and felt sick. She could still hear the shriek ringing in her ears and see the eyes locked on hers. She looked up into a mirror.

Her eyes—my eyes.

She startled back with the realization that those eyes were not so unlike hers.

Danny came back in with water and cookies in hand and saw she looked very upset.

"What's wrong?" he asked, suddenly worried.

"This pocket watch," she said, picking it back up, "who did it belong to?"

"Oh, that old thing? Umm, I think it was a great-great—shoot, I don't know how many greats—grandfather," he said, scratching his head. "He was our oldest family member here. He started up our legacy with farming."

Evelyn felt even more sick. So her boyfriend's however-many-greats great-grandfather was a murderer! She must have looked awful.

"Do you feel okay, babe? Should I take you home?" He was worried—poor guy had no idea of what she just saw.

She shook her head, trying to get out of the fog and come back to her reality.

"No. I'm fine. Just curious."

For some reason, she didn't feel she should or could tell him about the arrowhead or the pocket watch.

He came over and closed the box and wrapped his arms around her waist and pulled her to him. She tried to fall back into him and get the blissful feeling she had just moments before, but her stomach felt in knots and her ears still had the piercing shriek in them. She closed her eyes and took a deep breath and turned around and just hugged Danny. She wanted to squeeze him tight as if to bring herself back into the present.

She rested her head on his strong shoulder and breathed deeply. He must have taken it as a sign of contentment because he relaxed, his still-naked body caressing her. He picked her face up toward him and kissed her and smiled at her, and she returned the smile.

Danny's shirt fell open, her bare breasts were back on his chest, and then he rose again to meet her. She giggled at the growing member between them.

"What?" he said innocently.

Danny pushed his shirt down off her shoulders and let it fall to the ground. Her mind was off the cabin now and only on Danny and his touch. The next thing she knew, she was on top of him.

She leaned down to kiss him and said, "Now isn't this a changeup?"

He smiled up at her and said, "But I like it."

Evey worked herself slowly down on him and took a sharp breath as he entered her again, but this time, she was on top and in control. She wasn't quite sure what to do, so she did what felt right to her. She felt sore, but she welcomed it—anything to keep her mind off what she had seen.

Danny was in ecstasy. She rode him as if he were a horse, moving her hip in the rhythm of a trot and squeezing him tight with her thighs. He thought he would blow at any minute with her breasts bouncing in his face. Then he did, when she took his hands in hers and put them on those gorgeous bouncing boobs. He grabbed her by the hips and pulled her down tight as he moaned and felt the wave of sensation all the way from his toes.

Evelyn was panting but clearly not as finished as he.

She slowly got off him, feeling sore between the legs. She wondered if doing it twice the first time was wise. Clearly, Danny wasn't bothered at all by that. He had a smile plastered on his face. She didn't think he would ever stop smiling.

"Babe, what time is it?" she asked.

His smile faded at thinking he would have her home late. He couldn't risk getting her in trouble and not being able to see her or do what they just did again for a long while if she was grounded.

"I'm not sure," he said.

Danny ran to the kitchen to look at the microwave clock. It was 11:30 p.m. He had thirty minutes to get her home. Midnight was the rule. She wasn't to start a new day without being home was the rule.

He threw her dress at her. "Get dressed, babe. We've only got thirty minutes, and it'll take twenty to get you home."

Danny and Evelyn pulled into her driveway at 11:56 p.m.—four minutes to spare. They took three of that four minutes to kiss in the moonlight just outside the back door and then walked in the house. Her grandparents were in the living room.

"Right on time like usual," her grandma said, smiling.

"I may not be very smart, but I'm smart enough to get my girl home on time so I can see her again," Danny said, winking at her grandma.

"How was the wedding?" Grandma asked, smiling.

"It was very elegant," Evey answered. "She had white roses with hints of pink, and they wrote their own vows."

"How sweet," said Grandma.

"What did they serve you to eat?" was all Grandpa wanted to know.

"Filet Mignon," replied Danny.

Grandpa clutched his chest and said, "Damn. Fancy meal and fancy price."

They all laughed.

"I'll walk you to the door, Danny," Evey said.

"See you at church tomorrow, Danny," chimed Grandma.

"Oh yes, ma'am. See you tomorrow," Danny said.

Evelyn felt guilty at the mention of church after what she had done twice that night before marriage. Danny must have sensed it because when they got to the back door, he kissed her cheek like always and whispered in her ear, "You don't need to worry. I plan on making an honest woman out of ya."

Evey slapped his arm and laughed. He pecked her real quick on the lips and jogged off to his truck, and she watched his taillights bump down the little gravel road and sighed.

Chapter 9

*E*velyn awoke to screams in her ears and those eyes looking at her. Tudley was startled too. She wondered if she had called out in her dreams.

"I'm sorry, Tudley. I'm having terrible dreams. I saw something I wish I wouldn't have. Let's go to our tree," she said, sliding on her house slippers.

She stepped lightly to not wake her grandparents and because she felt a little sore. She touched her neck, remembering Danny's touch, and smiled a little. But her mind was racing with the visions she had seen when she held the old pocket watch in her hand.

She let herself and Tudley out of the back door as quietly as she could. She never felt scared when he was with her. He always let her know if something bad was around and had even fought another coyote to defend her honor. She smiled at her "dog."

They made their way across the back to her tree. She made it to the trunk of the tree and slid her slippers off. She needed her toes to help grasp where she was going. Evelyn made it up to her branch and let out a breath and let her head fall against the trunk of the tree. Tudley lay on her slippers at the base of the tree on guard.

Evey stayed there, just thinking, trying to piece together everything. She looked up at the full moon, so bright and beautiful.

If I were a wolf, I'd howl, she laughed to herself.

She heard the owls as if to answer her own thoughts. They were hooting. She decided to hoot back. She didn't know why, but it felt right.

Dang, am I talking with them about who was going to die? she wondered. *Oh well.*

"Did you know about the three people in my vision?" she asked aloud. "Were you trying to tell me about them?"

The owls went silent.

"I wish you could tell me who they were and if their deaths count as the three if it already happened," she kept wondering out loud, but now to silence.

They didn't hoot again that night. Grandma was watching Evey from the kitchen window. She was quiet, but she just sensed when her granddaughter got up. She had been watching her go to that very tree during nights when she had trouble sleeping. Grandma wondered what bothered her baby girl that night. She could see she was talking, maybe to Tudley or maybe just out loud to clear her thoughts and work through them.

Grandma had heard the owls too and knew Evey heard them. She had seen her look in the direction from which it came. The owls seemed to be following her granddaughter, and she said a silent prayer of protection around Evelyn that these owls weren't there to foretell of her going. She could not bear losing another daughter.

What must have been at least an hour later, Evey climbed down the tree to put her warm slippers on.

"Thank you, Tudley, for keeping my slippers safe." Evey scratched his ears.

The coyote yawned and stretched.

"I'm ready for bed now. Let's go," she said, and Tudley followed.

They quietly came back in, and Evey almost jumped out of her skin when she saw her grandma at the kitchen table.

"I didn't mean to scare you, honey," Grandma said sympathetically.

"Oh, it's okay, Grandma. I'm sorry. I couldn't sleep."

"Do you want to talk about it? I know you've had a lot happen lately," Grandma said in her understanding way.

Evey sighed all the way from her toes and rubbed her temples. She walked to the table and sat down.

"Grandma, I saw something else tonight. I'm not sure but I think Danny's ancestors are murderers, and they are somehow tied to our family."

Grandma looked startled at that.

"Why do you think that, sweetie?" she prodded.

"Well, I held an old pocket watch, and it was Danny's great-something's, and I saw him burn a little, old cabin down with people inside—a baby, a father, and a mother. And . . . and the mother was so sick and in bed and looked at him from the flames, Grandma. She stared him right in the eye as she died, and it was the most odd feeling that I got. I looked into her eyes, and they were my eyes. Not like I was seeing through her eyes, but my eyes—the same color and shape. And she was so familiar like I knew her in my very being."

"And you're wondering how this ties in with the arrowhead and the boy and the little girl?" Grandma finished Evey's thought.

Evey nodded. She was glad Grandma didn't ask where she touched the pocket watch. She never could hide the truth from her, and she wasn't ready for her to know those details. These were bad enough.

Evey made her way to bed. Tudley was already asleep. He didn't move as she climbed into bed. Her body ached from tiredness. She prayed the dreams would stop so she could sleep. The burden of knowing when someone was going to die may be better than seeing it, even if it did happen a million years ago. She yawned and stretched and rolled to her side to make her nest.

She did find sleep but dreamt of Indian songs. She didn't feel scared or anxious but at peace hearing the drums and the chants of an ancient tongue. She knew it was her Indians. She slept. It was as if they kept the bad visions away so she could sleep.

She was grateful, and when she awoke, Evey said a quiet thank-you to singers and drum players of her dreams as she looked out the window at the magnolia tree to see a little cardinal perched high up singing a song. Grandma had also told her, when a cardinal comes to see you, it's someone who has died coming to see you, and Evey always thought of her mom when she had one visit. She whispered another silent thank-you.

Chapter 10

It was a typical Sunday morning. Evelyn got on a nice T-shirt-style dress and sandals and headed toward the kitchen. She could smell breakfast sausage and knew Grandpa was cooking. He always made Sunday breakfast so Grandma could have a morning off to get ready and primp for church.

She walked into the kitchen to see her grandpa swaying back and forth at the little gas stove, singing an Elvis tune.

"Oh, Elvis, shake your pelvis!" Evey hooted toward her grandpa who whizzed around and wiggled his eyebrows and more laboriously shook his hips.

She put her hands to her eyes and laughed hard from her belly. She walked to the stove and pecked him on the cheek and took a peek at what he was cooking up.

About the same time, Grandma stepped in the kitchen, laughing. She had heard the ruckus. Those two always kept her on her toes and rolling with laughter. Grandma looked really nice. She had on a nice floral print dress with a red shawl around her shoulders, her pearls, and her fire-engine red lipstick to match. Not everyone can really pull off that shade of red, but Grandma could.

Being the smart man he was, Grandpa took note, "I'm going to hate to mess your lipstick up with my sausage."

"Grandpa!" Evey shouted with a terrible look on her face.

"What? I am cooking breakfast sausage," he said with a sneaky smirk on his face.

Grandma laughed and went and kissed him on the cheek.

"I'm two for two!" Grandpa said, waving his spatula in the air triumphantly.

Grandma looked confused.

"Both my pretty girls kissed me on the cheek this morning," he said, giving her a way overstated wink.

Evey chuckled and poured her and her grandma a cup of coffee.

"How are you feeling this morning, honey?" Grandma asked Evey.

"I'm feeling a little tired but better. I still had dreams, but they were peaceful. It seemed like they were keeping the bad ones away," she said looking past to somewhere else.

"Who was keeping them away?" Grandma asked curiously.

"I think the Indians—my Indians. They were singing and playing drums. I didn't see any of them, just could hear them and I slept," she explained, still feeling comfort thinking of it.

"It's this place. You know we all have dreams sometimes. They must like you." Grandma said, smiling and nodding.

And at that, Grandpa was plopping down a breakfast of pan sausage, pancakes, and eggs.

"Yummy!" Evey said, filling up her plate.

They rode to church, and Evey still sat in the middle of her grandparents in the old truck. It was a little more snug these days but still a comfort to be there secure. Her grandpa said he will always have that truck because he could still work on it and wasn't like the new stuff these days that you always have to take into the shop.

Their little family pulled into church, and she got out smiling to see Danny waiting on her. He always waited in front of the church for her to steal a kiss before they went in to sit with their families and hear the sermon. They always sat separate with their families, not wanting to upset them. She was smiling too.

"Looks like someone is happy to see you this morning and looking quite handsome too," Grandma teased, nudging the young lady.

Evey laughed and said, "He is a looker for sure."

They walked toward him and the church. Danny was smart. He shook her grandpa's hand first, hugged her grandma, and then lastly kissed Evelyn on the cheek.

Danny looked her grandpa in eye and, with his arm wrapped about Evey's shoulder, asked, "May I sit with Evelyn this morning during the service?"

His face was turning a little pink.

Grandpa was taken aback at first but then straightened and said, "Son, I see no problem with it, if that's where you want to sit."

Evelyn must have had her mouth open because her grandma said, smiling with pride, "Close your mouth, dear. You shouldn't be surprised that he would want to sit beside the girl he loves."

"Danny, what about your parents? Won't they be upset if you sit with me instead of them?" Evelyn asked with a worried look on her face and her brows furrowed.

"Well, I imagine they will have to get over it. What is it that the preacher says, that a man shall leave his parents and be joined with his wife?"

"There's just the one problem—I'm not your wife," Evelyn chuckled, squeezing his arm.

"You will be, and besides we've already joined," he replied back with a boyish grin.

Evey turned bright red and laughed a little and just said, "Okay, sit by me then and be ready for the stares."

Stares they got. It felt as if the whole church was looking at them, and she felt like she could feel Danny's mother's stare on the back of her head. It didn't seem to bother Danny at all. He gave her a reassuring smile and put his arm around her on the pew.

Grandpa, Grandma, Evey, and then Danny sat in one pew. Some parishioners seemed shocked, and some looked with tenderness at the young love. Evelyn felt a little guilty about what they had done just the night before and where they were now sitting, but she didn't regret it. She leaned in a little closer toward him so that at least their sides would touch. But they couldn't show too much affection in church. She felt him giggle a little and give her a side glance. She just smiled and looked down. What a sweet romance. Her grandpa looked down a few times to make sure their display was completely appropriate, which it was.

The service ended, and they all got up to walk out together. They got to the door to shake their little bald preacher's hand.

"I noticed you were sitting with Evelyn today, Danny."

"I think everyone noticed, sir," Danny said with a smile.

"Well, son, it appears as if you two are serious now. Keep in account what the Lord says of relationships," the preacher said, eyeing Danny.

"I will, sir. That's one of the reasons I've decided to sit by her from now on. If we want to be together, we should hear the Lord's word together," Danny replied like a cunning fox.

He was brilliant and always knew what to say. Evey just tightened her grasp around his arm approvingly.

The preacher clasped Evey's hand and said, "Always a pleasure. my dear."

"Yes, preacher. I sure enjoyed the bit about eternal bonds," Evey said, smiling so sweetly at him.

He stiffened a bit at this and then smiled and nodded them off.

Danny's parents were in fact shocked that he sat with Evelyn and her grandparents. They stopped the two short of his truck. Danny always took Evey home after church and had lunch with her family.

"Danny, you know you could have just asked Evey to sit with us?" his mother said in her ever-so-indignant voice.

"Yes, son. That would have been more appropriate," Chimed in his father.

Danny raised an eyebrow at this, and Evelyn just held his arm tight in her grasp to try to steal him from saying something he shouldn't.

"More appropriate? How so?" he asked, looking from his mother to his father.

"Son, we are a family, and we would just like you to sit with us. It was somewhat embarrassing that you just sat with them without saying a word to us. And besides, isn't it your name she will be taking if you should get married?"

The *if* rang in Evelyn's ears, and she felt flustered by their acting like their family was better than hers just because they have money. Her face was burning with anger.

"Oh yes. It is my name she will be taking, and it's for me she will be taking it, not for what it stands for or how much money is behind it, but because she loves me. What's embarrassing is you even having this conversation. I would hope to think that you would know you raised me right and that I am smart and capable enough to pick a woman worthy of me," Danny said through clenched teeth.

"Danny, that's not what we meant. Yes we can see you two are so in love, but you're young, and it's just not proper that you would go sit with her family instead of your own," his mother interceded.

"Well, aren't you just the hypocrite? I think it's time you read Ephesians again—'For this reason a man will leave his father and mother and be united to his wife, and the two shall become one flesh.' Ephesians 5:31," Danny said standing taller.

They hadn't much to say after that, but Evelyn beamed with pride.

"And in case you didn't know, Mom, Dad, I plan to make Evelyn my wife as soon as she'll have me. I've loved her from the start, and I do not plan on living life without her," Danny finished off.

His mom's mouth dropped open, and his dad said, "Son, I do not fault you for this choice. Your mother and I are headed home. Be home by eight this evening."

He grabbed Danny's mother by the arm and ushered her off.

"Danny, I can't believe that you said that to your parents!" Evelyn blurted out.

"What? The truth? Dammit, Evey, I love you, and to damn with them if they can't see that. You are who I want," he said with conviction.

Her heart felt like it would burst. She needed his touch, but they were still in the parking lot of the church and her grandparents were expecting them shortly behind them for lunch.

"Danny, I do love you," she said as she firmly grasped him around his waist and hugged him, laying her head on his shoulder.

He kissed the top of her head and said, "I love you too."

They got in his truck, and she slid into the middle, giggling as she thought about the night before. And as she had put his hand in between her thighs, she had the urge to do it again.

"What are you giggling about?" he asked.

"I was just thinking," she said.

"About what?" he asked, already knowing the answer.

"I was just thinking about last night and, well, all of it," she said, blushing.

He kissed her on the cheek and said, "Let's get out of here."

They did, and he drove a little slower toward the farm, letting his hand rest on her thigh. He wanted to touch her badly, and she him. He looked over at her to see her smiling, looking out of the window. She glanced at him and smiled. She put her hand on his thigh in question. He grasped her hand and put it to himself and clutched tightly.

She relaxed her hand on his member and was extremely gentle as she caressed him into a standing position.

He made a noise in the back of his throat.

"You aren't going to wreck, are you?" Evey asked with a smile on her face.

"I don't plan to," he said with a crooked grin.

"Good," she said as she unzipped his fly.

Within a few seconds, she had his pants undone, and her hand grasped firmly but gently around him, and he moaned as she stroked him.

She wanted in on the fun too.

"Take the other back road," she whispered in his ear as she bit it.

He did, and once he turned onto the road and they got out of other cars' view, she pulled her dress up and straddled him while he was driving.

"Can you still see the road?" she asked.

"Yes, but oh my. Oh, I don't know if I can keep my foot on the gas," he said back.

"But you have to. We can't be gone too much longer than necessary or they'll come looking for us," she said as she started bouncing up and down as they drove down the old back road.

She knew it wouldn't take long—and they couldn't—seeing as they had to be at lunch soon. She thrust down on him hard and as deep as she could let him in and let out a shriek of ecstasy. He liked that. He had one hand on the wheel and the other hand on her hip, pulling her down onto him as far as she could go. One, two, three more thrusts up from him, and he was panting hard and she was out of breath.

"Oh my. That was fun, but I didn't think about the mess," she said, looking at him still on his lap as he was still creeping down the road.

He got a nervous look and said, "Get in the glove box. I have some napkins in there."

She leaned over with him still inside her to open the glove box, "Ahhh . . . oh," he yelped.

"What's wrong?" she asked, feeling scared.

"Nothing," he laughed. "I'm just sensitive . . . you know . . . after."

They made it to the little, white farmhouse, and she smiled at him mischievously; and he just laughed and shook his head.

"I have my hands full with you," he said.

"Your hands or your lap?" she questioned, wiggling her eyebrows at him and grabbing his hand.

He shook his head again and laughed even harder.

They could smell lunch from the porch. Porkchops, green beans, squash, and fried potatoes—everything smelled great. Everyone was in heaven.

"Grandma, you really outdid yourself this time," Danny said to her while rubbing his stomach.

She smiled. "Oh, it was nothing, dear."

"C'mon, let's do the dishes," said Evey, nudging Danny.

He slowly got up and went to the sink to help her.

"I'll wash, you dry," she told him, handing him a towel.

Evelyn was looking out the window at her tree as she methodically washed the dishes, and her mind was wandering to the visions she had seen. She seemed far off. Danny must've have been watching her.

"What are you thinking about, babe?" he asked.

"What? Oh, I . . . well"—she looked at her grandma—"I'm not really sure. I was just staring at my tree."

She at Grandma again. She wondered if she could tell Danny the truth in time.

"You and your tree," he said. "I'm almost jealous of it."

"It is a special place for me," she said, meaning it.

Grandma came over to help.

"Here, Danny. Hand me that dish, and I'll put it away."

Grandma swooped in when she needed her.

Evelyn contemplated what Danny would say if she told him just about the arrowhead, not necessarily the pocket watch.

How do you tell someone murderers run in your family? she mused. *Not my Danny though. He's as close to perfect as you could get.*

Chapter 11

Danny walked with Evelyn to go check the calf. She didn't really need to check the calf but wanted any excuse to just be alone with Danny. They walked hand in hand down the little dirt path—not saying anything, just being together. They got out to pen and knew no one from the house could see them. Danny pinned her up against a post on the fence and kissed her hard.

"I love you," he said, looking into her eyes.

She got on tiptoe and kissed him gently and told him, "I love you too, Danny."

She pressed her forehead on his, trying to will him to see what was going on inside her head.

The calf mooed, and she turned her gaze to the little girl.

"Hey, you. Do you need some lovin' too?" she asked in a baby voice, pulling away from Danny and climbing through the fence.

She got in with the baby and was scratching her head and cooing to her.

"I've already been replaced by a cow," Danny said in fake despair.

"She is cute," she said back, teasing.

She thought a while and asked, "Danny, do you just like stuff because I do?"

He looked scared like this was a loaded question.

"Well, I really like you, so I'll do my best to like whatever you do," he answered.

Good answer, she thought. *But is that the right one?*

He held her hand as she climbed back through the fence. She got tripped up a little and fell forward, and naturally Danny caught her.

"I'll always catch you when you, fall baby," he said.

She laughed and kissed his cheek.

"Do we have to walk back?" he asked, already knowing the answer.

"I wish we didn't, but you know we should," she answered.

"Well then, first . . ." he said as he swung her up in his embrace and grabbed her bottom and fit his mouth on hers.

He kissed her and grabbed her for what seemed like a long time.

"Whew, I think that may tide me over for a bit," she said as she planted a kiss on his nose.

He laughed and sat her down.

"I don't think anything could ever tide me over, but I sure do like to think about all the things we've been doing together," he said, making Evey blush.

"I just can't help it," she said. "I just want you."

And he kissed her again and then sighed and took her hand as they headed back up the path to the house.

When they got back to the house, they could smell cookies. They both smiled, excited about cookies.

When they came in, Grandpa said, "I think y'all have been sweet enough on each other that you don't need any cookies. They are all mine!"

"Oh my gosh, Grandpa! You better share," Evey hollered at him.

"There's nothing sweeter than Evey, but I could settle for a cookie," Danny said.

Grandma smiled and tossed him a cookie.

"Yes! Thank you, Grandma!"

Evey went over and hugged Grandma and stole a cookie. Grandma smelled her and eyed her suspiciously, and Evelyn just smiled at her. She knew she smelled like Danny but hoped no one would make a comment. They sat at the kitchen table together, sharing a glass of milk to dip their giant chocolate-chip cookies in. They were so content, until Danny realized he needed to get home.

"I'll walk you to your truck," Evey told Danny.

Grandma put a few cookies in a bag to take home.

Danny smiled at her and told her, "You're the best."

"Well, you don't think Grandpa likes me only for my good looks, do you now?" Grandma asked, teasing.

Everyone laughed and Grandpa said, "Those good looks caught me, and those cookies kept me."

He and grandma kissed, and Evey smiled as Danny put his arm around her. Evey didn't get the grossed-out feeling like a lot of kids did when they saw their parents being sweet with each other. She felt so contented and happy to see them love each other so much.

She took Danny by the hand and led him out to his truck.

Danny bent and put his head on her shoulder.

"I hate this part. I don't want to leave you. I want to go inside and go to bed with you and hold you all night," he told Evey.

"I know. I want the same," she sighed.

"One day, I'm going to marry you, and we will never say goodbye again," he said, and he kissed her.

He opened his truck door to get in, and Evey spotted the napkins.

"Hey, don't forget to get rid of the evidence when you get home."

He looked at her, confused.

"The napkins. We sure don't need your mom to find those after you stood her up to sit with me in church."

He laughed.

"I was going to keep them like a souvenir."

She hit his arm. "Gross!"

She made a face and laughed some more.

"I love you, and I'll get us back to the camp house soon. Just you and me and I'm going to explore you completely. I want to memorize every inch of you," he said staring contently at her face.

The mention of the camp house made her shiver.

"Or maybe you could get me to the fishing hole with some snacks and quilt?" she eyed him, questioning.

"It doesn't sound as comfortable, but whatever you want, babe," he said to her and kissed her once more and finally got into his truck.

She shut his door and stepped back so he could leave. She watched his taillights disappear down the road and felt sad at his leaving but was okay.

Evelyn walked back into the house to see her Grandma smiling wide at her.

"Were you watching us through the window, Grandma?" she asked.

"Me? Heavens no. I'd never do that," she said in an unconvincing voice.

"So you saw us smooching then, huh?" Evey laughed.

"Sweetheart, I would say you'd have to be smooching to have been together for so long and him to sit with us in church today. He really does plan on marrying you," Grandma stated.

Evey smiled at that. "Yes, and he told his mother as much."

Grandma raised an eyebrow. "Oh, did he now? Tell me everything."

Evelyn did tell her grandma everything. She told her how Danny stood up to his mom for her and even quoting scripture to her. Grandma smiled and enjoyed hearing all the details.

When Evey finished, she went and took a shower to wash all the day's activities off her and went to bed Tudley in tow. The owls were extremely talkative in the magnolia tree. Evey got up and opened the window, and she just listened. She didn't know why, but felt she should listen.

They looked at her, and she at them. Never actually uttering a word, she asked them what they wanted.

I know it's silly, Evey chastised herself, *but they've been around for days now. I wonder if they have a nest in the tree. That would be a perfectly reasonable explanation for them being there so many nights in a row.*

That night, she didn't feel upset by their presence; she felt at peace with it. She figured she just must let it come if it will. Finally, she shut her window and went to bed and said a prayer again.

"I know I hear you, and if you're listening, please play your drums and sing your music that I may sleep again," she prayed.

And she slept with echoes of drums in her ears.

Chapter 12

Oh Monday morning, you come with so much to be done. Grandpa and Evelyn got started at daylight patching the fence and other things that needed to be done. School would be starting in a few hours, and they needed to get all the major things done before then. They would finish the rest when Evey got home.

They fixed the windmill and a hole in the hay barn. Grandpa would make new laying boxes for the hens while she was gone, and when she would get home, they would shred pasture and fill in potholes on their road. Evey was very tired at the end of every day and missed Danny in the process. They would see each other on Wednesday at church, but her mind kept being preoccupied with thoughts of the Indians and the people murdered. She needed to find out what happened, but how? Which Indians were even here?

At the end of the day when they were done working, Evey stole away to her tree to think. She kicked her boots and socks off, enjoying the freedom and the feel of grass on her bare feet after the long workday, and climbed up her tree. She made it to her branch and sat with her back against the truck. She always swore she could feel the life in the tree, but everyone just laughed at her. She surveyed the woods where the little stream was. That's were her Indian boy was working on his arrowhead.

"Who were you?" she asked aloud.

The wind blew her hair in tangles around her face as if to answer, but she didn't understand. She just thought the breeze felt nice.

Evey was so lost in her thoughts on who he was and how to find out that she didn't notice the truck coming up the driveway. She had her eyes closed and head back on the trunk when she was suddenly brought back into the realm of the living when she heard a familiar voice.

"Hey, babe," Danny said from the ground.

Her eyes flew open, and she looked down with a smile on her face to see her man.

"Danny!" she yelped with glee, scurrying down the tree into his arms. "I didn't know you were coming by today."

He smiled. "I couldn't keep away."

"You were just with me all day yesterday, you know?" she questioned him.

They were smiling at each other.

"Oh my gosh, Danny. I'm sure I stink after working!" she said, mortified.

He whiffed her and shrugged, "You've smelled better."

She ran inside, and Danny was not far behind her.

Grandma was in the kitchen cooking and looked up to see her granddaughter come by in a blur and Danny behind her.

"What in the world?" Grandma wondered aloud.

"Evey stinks after working today and is upset I smelled her," Danny said, snickering.

"Oh. Makes sense," Grandma said and continued working on her meatloaf. "Are you staying for supper. Danny?"

"If that's okay with you," he replied, and she nodded with a genuine smile.

She knew that his presence would make Evey happy.

Evelyn was in the shower in a flash, scrubbing away. The water was hitting her closed eyes when she had a thought.

I need to go to the museum!

She knew they had information on all the local tribes and maybe she could find something out. She would ask Danny to take her soon.

He'd probably hate it, but the lure of some alone time with me might seal the deal, she argued with herself.

She got out of the shower and put on some cotton shorts and a tank top and headed out the bathroom door.

She found everyone in the kitchen. Danny looked up from the table where he was snapping green beans for Grandma and smiled really big. He didn't always get to see that much of her legs, and he liked it. She went and sat by him and began to help snap green beans with him. They kept brushing hands on purpose, and at one point, he dropped a bean so that he would have to go under the table to get it. He kissed her high on the thigh on his way back up. Evey eyed him. She couldn't handle him doing stuff like that behind her grandma's back.

"Oh, I was telling your grandma while you were in the shower that my mom wants you over for dinner tomorrow. It seems me sitting with you in church has her wanting to visit with you more," Danny said.

"Okay. I hope she isn't too mad."

They finished snapping beans, and then Evey said she was going to shut the chickens and go check the windmill one more time before supper to make sure it was still turning and pumping water.

Their windmill—or, actually, windpump would be the proper term—was essentially a wind-powered water pump to fill cow troughs. Grandpa seemed grateful to not have to get up to go back out. He was very tired.

"Don't worry, if it isn't working, I'll send Danny up to fix it," Evey said, laughing.

Danny gave her a look, but he was happy they could steal away together, for a little while at least.

Evelyn got the chickens shut, and they headed down the little dirt path to go past the cow pen to get to the windmill. She and Danny held hands the whole way.

"Are your parents okay with you being here again today?" she asked.

"Probably not, but I told them I was going to marry you, so it's only right we spend as much time together as possible, and I told them I'd bring you to dinner tomorrow."

She smiled at him.

They made it over to the windmill, and it was still turning. Evey let out a sigh of relief.

Danny was staring at her, and she looked at him and said, "What?"

"I was just thinking how beautiful you are and how badly I want to pin you up against something and have my way with you," he blurted out, turning red.

"Well then, aren't you quite the Honest Abe tonight?" she teased.

He pulled her to him and put his mouth on hers and kissed her deeply. Her whole body was tingling, and she did want him. He slid his hand down the waistband of her cotton shorts and found she was ready for him.

He looked at her and told her, "I must have you. Please?"

Evelyn took him by the hand and led him over to the other side of the calf pen. No one would see there, other than the cows. She wished she could lie with him, but she was clean and having dirt and grass smeared all along her or him would be a dead giveaway. She pressed him up against the side of the calf shed and kissed him and groped down to grab him. He took a deep breath, and she looked into his eyes.

"I want you so badly, but I don't necessarily want splinters in my rear, so what's your plan?" she asked.

He didn't have one. All he knew was his carnal need for her was at the foremost part of his brain. He looked around.

Damn, what should I do? he thought.

Finally, without another thought, he took her hand and put it down his pants and told her, "We will do it together, okay?"

She nodded as he penetrated her with his fingers. They let their hands dance on each other and do the talking. But she wanted more.

She stopped him, and he looked puzzled at her. He didn't understand.

"I want all of you," she said.

"But you said you didn't—"

"All of you," Evey interrupted.

Danny let instinct take over. He ripped her shorts down and turned her around, held on to her hips, and thrust hard into her from behind. She moaned.

"Shhh," he said as he thrust as deep as he could go, and she quivered.

He liked that. He didn't want to make love to her; he wanted to own her in that moment, and he thrust harder and harder and faster and faster until you could hear the slaps of flesh on flesh. When he finished, he was shaking and breathing so hard, the fog cleared from his mind.

"I'm so sorry. I didn't mean to . . . I don't know what got into me," he stammered out.

Evey turned to look at him and said, "I never told you to stop."

"I didn't hurt you did I?"

"No you didn't. I would have told you to stop if you were hurting me. In fact, I liked it very much. Now we need to pull it together and go in and eat supper," Evelyn said, realizing how tired she was.

They made their way back to the house to eat, and their meal was as usual—delicious. Danny loved eating at her house. She even managed to talk Danny into taking her to the museum, but what after happened at the pen, she was pretty sure she could ask anything of him right now.

Her eyes went to the blue medicine bottle, and her grandma followed her gaze and looked at her thoughtfully.

"What are you looking at?" Danny asked.

"That medicine bottle up there," she answered.

He looked confused.

"I found an arrowhead the other day while working. That's why I want you to take me to the museum. I want to research what kind of Indians were here."

"But don't go telling the museum nerds nothing!" Grandpa butted in her. "I don't want them tearing the whole place up looking for broken pottery."

Evey smiled, and Danny laughed.

"The secret is safe with me. I'd much rather nap than go to the museum, but I'll do anything for Evey," said Danny.

Grandma was still looking at Evey. She was wondering if she would tell Danny about the visions. She thought she should before they got in too deep together or had they already? She studied her granddaughter. She hoped, for her sake, not. To love someone and find out they can't love all of you would be devastating. She never had to worry about that with Evey's grandpa. He always just loved them all for everything they were.

52

Chapter 13

Evey put on a pair of clean gray slacks and a white blouse to go to Danny's for dinner. He was at her house on time as usual. Danny pulled in at 5:30 p.m., and Grandma walked her to the door to see her off.

"Sweetheart, why don't you think about telling him about your visions tonight?" Grandma said. "If you're going to dinner with his family, it seems you're getting serious."

"I'll think about it, Grandma," she told her and squeezed her hands.

Danny got out of the truck to come to the door to get her. He was at least a gentleman, Grandma noted, but her sense of unease was rising. Throughout the years, she had learned to pay attention to the sense of her blood tingling right under the skin when something was amiss.

She looked at her granddaughter and said, "I love you. Keep your wits about you, okay?"

Evey gave her a look and nodded. Evey knew when to take her fun-loving grandma seriously.

Danny's house was just a few miles down the road. He pulled through a fancy gate with a calligraphy *B* on it and made his way down the tree-lined limestone driveway to a fancy red-brick home with two chimneys at either end. Evey always wondered why on Earth they needed two chimneys in Southern Texas, but it sure was pretty.

Danny parked, got out, and walked around the truck to let Evey out.

He looked her up and down and nodded and said, "You look good, like a lady."

"Do I not always look like a lady to you?" she said, acting as if he upset her.

They both laughed, and he said, "Lady you are not, my dear, and I'm okay with that. But my mother . . . well, I told her to play nice tonight."

Evey just eyed him, and he walked her into the grand home.

They walked through huge wooden doors into an elegant entryway studded with a crystal chandelier hanging from the ceiling.

Danny's mother walked through her sitting room to greet them.

"Evelyn darling, come in!" she said overly sweet and hugging her quite tightly.

"Thank you for having me over, Mrs. Bailey," Evey said.

"Oh dear. It's nothing. If you and Danny are to be together, we need to groom you into a proper lady, and you need to learn to host dinner parties. I want you to be my shadow tonight," Mrs. Bailey demanded her.

Evey looked at Danny, and he shrugged his shoulders.

"It's sounds like fun," Evey said. "Let's do this."

Evey felt a tinge of unease. She was more of an outside working girl, not an inside hostess.

Mrs. Bailey took Evey by the arm and took her into the sitting room where all the county's finest were seated. She introduced her to the double-chinned county judge, Judge Barley; his wife Judy; and their twin daughters, Hailey and Sailey.

Then she introduced her to the rest of the who's who, and one lady, Mrs. Langston, told Mrs. Bailey, "What a charming girl. Is this Danny's girlfriend you were telling me about?"

"Why, yes indeed," Mrs. Bailey spoke up.

"She looks quite lovely. You shouldn't have any issues turning her into one of us," said Mrs. Langston.

Evey felt sick to her stomach. She didn't want to be changed into something she didn't even want to be. She listened to the ladies gossip and watched the men sip fine whiskey and smoke cigars on the screened-in porch and longed for her home where life made sense to her. She couldn't let her guard down here, and everyone seemed to be putting on a show.

"What do you think, Evelyn?" Mrs. Bailey said, which made Evey jump in surprise.

"I'm sorry, what did you ask?" Evey said.

"Darling, we were asking you what your plans are after graduation?" Mrs. Bailey said, looking none too pleased that Evey wasn't paying attention to her and her friends.

"Oh. I plan on going to A&M to study animal medicine. I intend on becoming a veterinarian. It would be a plus on the farm, and the added bonus is, I love working with the cattle," Evey said, her face brightening as she talked of what she wanted to be.

The ladies erupted in laughter, startling Evey.

"Dear me, no. You can't be serious. You don't have to work if you marry into the Bailey family. Women shouldn't do such messy work anyway. You've got a lot to learn about the lifestyle of a Bailey woman," Mrs. Bailey said.

The more Evey thought about it, the more she wasn't sure if she wanted to be a Bailey woman—full of fake smiles and gossip. At one point, Mrs. Bailey took her by the hand to head into the kitchen, which was as large as the farmhouse itself. Evey thought her grandma would love such a big kitchen.

"Now, Evelyn, part of hosting dinner parties is deciding your menu and coming in here to check that everything is just as it should be."

Evey nodded at Mrs. Bailey, feeling numb.

A nice older Mexican man with gray hair turned around from the stove and smiled.

"Mrs. Bailey, everything is almost done," he said in a heavy accent.

"Hi, I'm Evelyn," Evey said, holding her hand out and walking toward the cook.

He looked shocked but returned her smile, shook her hand, and said, "I am Juan, Miss Evelyn. Mucho gusto."

"Tambien a te," Evey said in Spanish in return, and Juan smiled even bigger.

"Evelyn, we don't mingle with the help. We are their employer, and we just tell them what to do, and you always find something wrong so you can go out to the dinner table and tell everyone else how you had to fix everything that was messed up," Mrs. Bailey said, looking appalled at her behavior.

Evey looked at Juan with a look of apology, and he gave her a brief nod.

Mrs. Bailey went on picking apart the wonderful appetizers right before her and Juan's eyes and then turned to go to the dining area.

Before she got all the way out, Evey turned around and apologized, "Yo siento, Juan."

Juan smiled and said, "It's okay, mija. It's a job, and I appreciate your kindness."

Evey couldn't stand being Mrs. Bailey's shadow. She was mean and treated her employees like they were beneath her. That is not how Evey was raised. Everyone had value, and every job counted. She really wished she had just stayed at home.

"I had to get Juan to fix the appetizers. He completely forgot the dill on the shrimp bites. I don't know what would happen if I didn't go around fixing everything," Mrs. Bailey said in fake exasperation, and all the ladies nodded at the table.

Evey looked over to find Danny laughing and enjoying himself with the men. He must have felt her eyes on him because he turned to smile at her and turned right back around to their company. Evey noticed that the men and women stayed separate at the party. She wanted Danny to whisk in and save her, but he never did.

The food was delicious. Juan came in to tell everyone what they were being served. It was a full-course meal. Evey thought it silly to have so much silverware to use, but at least she knew to work her way in. You could tell they didn't wash their own dishes.

The big entrée was roasted mutton with garlic potatoes, asparagus, and roasted onions. It was wonderful. Evey didn't talk and ate her entire plate. The women looked at her in horror. Evey didn't understand and then looked at their plates. They had just taken a few bites of their food and apparently women weren't supposed to eat like men.

Danny was laughing, and so were the men.

"I told you the girl can eat," he said elbowing his dad.

Evey just gave him a death stare.

"Well, my grandmother says the best compliment you can give a cook is to clean your plate," Evey said, and the whole table erupted in laughter, laughing at her.

"Oh, dear. Ladies don't eat like that," Mrs. Langston said.

Evey had to bite her lip to keep from saying something she shouldn't. She shot a glance at Danny, and for once, he looked sorry at the situation.

Juan walked back in to bring dessert.

Evey stood up before he could announce desert and said, "Juan, gracias para la comida. Estas muy delicioso. Thanks for the food, it was delicious," staring right at Mrs. Bailey.

She would thank the help. Danny's mouth gaped open, and he got up to follow Evey as she walked to the porch.

She heard the judge say behind her as she walked out, "Man, she's a feisty one. I see what draws Danny to her."

Danny grabbed Evey by the arm and said, "Evey, c'mon now. They were just poking fun."

Evey glared at him. "Well, I don't call that fun, Danny. I hate the way your mom treats Juan! I hate the gossip, the fake smiles, and I hate that they think I shouldn't go to school and get a job."

Danny took a deep breath. "Evey, you don't have to work, and this is how my family operates. They throw dinner parties and entertain the elites of our county. It's good for business."

"Danny, I will go to college, and I will work, and I will not pretend to like a bunch of people I don't," Evey said, her face burning with anger.

He just stared at her, not sure what to say next.

"Evey, my mom will expect you to be the lady of the house and to be able to run it and run it well," Danny spoke carefully.

"Oh yeah, and what do you expect of me, Danny? I've never pretending to be something I'm not. That's what this was for your mom, huh? To show you and everyone else I can't be a Bailey woman?" she asked, getting angrier.

"No. Evey. I like you the way you are, but if we want my family's support, you've got to try," he said.

"I don't ask you to be anything you're not, Danny. Why aren't you doing the same for me? We can make our own way," she said, tears filling her eyes.

He just hugged her and said, "I'm sorry."

He would say whatever he needed to stop what Evey was feeling. He could work on her in the meantime.

"Come back inside with me, Evey, and tell everyone goodbye."

She nodded, ready to be out of there.

They went back in, and everyone got quiet and stared as they walked back in. Evey got very uncomfortable.

"We are sorry we caused a disruption at dinner," Danny said. "Please forgive us. Evey is getting used to be being with a Bailey man."

Evey wasn't sorry, and she was mad he apologized when she did nothing wrong. She just stood still with a stern look. Juan looked in from a side door and tried to give her an encouraging smile.

"All is forgiven, children," Mrs. Bailey said, looking at Evey.

Evey stood straighter and looked her directly in her gray eyes. Evey wouldn't dare be the first to break the glance, and Danny cleared his throat.

"Let's retire to the game room," Mrs. Bailey said, and everyone got up and followed her.

They walked through a long hall with paintings all down it. Evey stopped dead still when she saw a man with fierce gray eyes standing up straight in a suit, holding a pocket watch. The pocket watch had the initials DVB on it, and Evey looked down at his boots.

Those black boots, Evey remembered. *Those boots kicked a man down in the burning cabin.*

She stood stark still and just stared, almost forgetting to breathe.

"Do you like that painting?" Mrs. Bailey asked, studying Evey.

"Who is this?" Evey asked.

"Well, that is the very first Bailey to live in our area. He was pivotal in clearing out the savages and making it safer for us, and he acquired a lot of our land to the east of the woods during the Indian wars. He is a strong man and such an example of what a Bailey man should be," Mrs. Bailey said so proudly.

"So this is your husband's ancestor?" Evey asked, trying to suppress her disgust.

It was crazy how this painting made her feel, almost as if the man were actually standing in front of her.

Mrs. Bailey laughed and almost sounded like a witch.

"Oh, goodness no. I'm his descendant. No one ever changes the Bailey name. My husband took my name. As old-fashioned as I am, my name wasn't up to be changed, not when it means so much. Bailey is the most prominent name in our area, and names mean something."

Evey was indeed shocked at this, but it made sense seeing their mean gray eyes and made sense that her ancestor would be a murderer.

"So what is this man's name?" Evey asked, wanting a name for the murderer.

"His name is Daniel Vincent Bailey. That's were Danny's name came from. I've always felt something looking at this painting and wanted to honor the man who started it all," said Mrs. Bailey, looking at Evey.

How much does she really know? Evey wondered. *Did she know he had singlehandedly almost wiped out an entire family? I bet she did. But Danny—he couldn't know. He's not the same as that man or his mother.*

Chapter 14

Danny took Evey home, and she didn't say much. He knew she was upset, but he wasn't sure what all for. His mother was a tough woman, but she was who she was and expected a lot out of Evey. He hugged her, and she walked in without him, and he left to go back home.

When he got home, his mother was waiting for him.

"Son, she will never do as the lady of the house. The way she talks to the help and eats like an animal. I just can't," she said.

"Mother, I love her. She will figure it all out," Danny said.

"Danny, you weren't to love her. This is business. You marry her, and we get her land too—the way it was supposed to have been from the beginning. The first Daniel was always upset about not getting their piece too. It's your job to do your part and secure the rest of our fortune. It's perfect for rice," she said.

"Mother, Evey will never let it be that. She loves the cattle. Is it not enough to just get the land back and let it be what it is?" Danny said, almost pleading.

He really did love Evelyn now. They were more than lovers. She was his best friend. What started out as a plan to get her land had made him see how great she actually was, and he loved her free spirit and it was refreshing to see a woman work hard.

Mrs. Bailey looked at her son for a long time.

"Son, how lucky are you to actually like who you are to marry? But do not forget, she is an Ermis, and they are not like us. They are not meant to be anything else but workers. Do not forget what your job in this is," she said and walked off.

Danny let out a sigh. His mother wasn't telling him everything. He understood that land was power and money but couldn't have it all—power, money, and the girl.

Danny went to his room and relived the evening. They were really hard on Evey. He wasn't sure if he could right this, and if he didn't, his mother would kill him. She has been plotting to get that land forever. Something happened in the past that left the land not in their hands. A sick family was there whom his great-great-great-great-grandfather tried to help, but they ended up dying in a house fire and found out years later one of the girls had survived and was living with savages.

That meant the land went to the man she married, and his family lost their grip on it just like that. The only living heir got the land, and she had a say in what would be done with it. The land wasn't farmed; instead, she got animals and kept the ways of the healer and the townsfolk despised her for her Indian ways even though she was white. His family had thought her to be crazy and never right in the head after so much time with the Indians. There was no telling what happened to the poor girl.

He thought maybe he should just tell Evey the truth and then decided better not to. She would be so mad and never speak to him again if she knew of the plan, and he couldn't risk losing her. He hoped she was okay.

He called her, and when she answered, he said, "I love you. I'm sorry about tonight. I don't need you to change. You be yourself. That's who I love, and I promise no more dinner parties."

She sighed and said, "I love you too, but I can't help but wonder if this is right. I do not like your mother, and she obviously doesn't like me. How are we to make this work?"

"One day at a time. I'll come get you tomorrow to take you to the museum as promised, and we will start there. How about that?" he asked, hopeful.

"That sounds like a good start. I'll see you tomorrow," she said.

Evey wasn't ready to give up on him. He had been a constant in her life for a long time, and after everything and giving him herself, she wasn't ready to let him go. She hoped she could love him through the misconceptions.

Evey told her grandma and grandpa about the evening at the Baileys'. Grandma was ready to go over there and give her a piece of her mind, but grandpa intervened.

"Now, dearest, it sounds like Evey handled it pretty well. I'm proud of her for being kind in the midst of such jerks."

"I am proud of you too," Grandma added, hugging her granddaughter. "I'm proud of you for being yourself and not trying to mold into what other people think you should be, for you were made to be you, not what someone thinks you should be."

"Danny better grow a pair and learn to take up for his lady. He quoted Ephesians the other day, and it says 'To leave thy father and mother,' not stay and let them treat your partner like trash. When you marry someone, you marry their family too. Just think about that. We won't tell you who to love but will try to get you to think about all the aspects of it. I love you, sister."

Evey sighed and nodded. "I'm not ready to give up yet after everything we've been through and shared. He said earlier we will take it one day at a time. I'm going to try."

Chapter 15

Danny took Evelyn to the museum, as promised. It was only awkward for a little while, and then they were back to normal. When it was just the two of them, things were good. They went to lunch first and then to the museum. He said he wouldn't be bored on a full stomach.

At the museum, they walked around reading about the history of the county, the first post office, the first jail, and finally a small exhibit on the local tribe, the Karankawa. They were tall and scary looking. Many had bones through their lips and ears.

She read on about them, "The Karankawa Indians were a group of tribes who lived along the Gulf of Mexico in what is today Texas. During the eighteenth century the Karankawa were at war with the Spaniards in Texas. They then fought unsuccessfully to stay on their land after it was opened to Anglo-American settlement. The last known Karankawa were killed or died out by the 1860s."

Evey's stomach sank.

How sad, she thought.

"So they are all dead," Danny said. "It says here they were cannibals. I guess it serves them right to be killed then. Eww."

He shook his shoulders as if to get something off of him.

Evey looked over the pictures again. She didn't see her Indian in them. He didn't look scary, and neither did the older man carrying the little girl. Evey tried to sort out her thoughts.

Evelyn went to the front desk and asked the round lady with short, red hair if they had any more information on the local Indians.

She pursed her lips together and said, "No we don't. There really just isn't much here, but our neighboring county museum has a larger exhibit. They have life-size replicas and a real photo of the last Karankawa alive in this region of Texas."

Evey got a little happier at that. It was so disheartening that a whole people was killed off. Obviously, Danny didn't care or have the same sentiment. He was ready to go.

"Look, babe, I love you more than life itself, but why don't you get your grandma to go with you to the next museum?" he said.

She laughed and nodded.

"What else do you need to know, Evey? You found an arrowhead, and now you've found out that there were Karankawa down here," Danny asked her.

Evey took a deep breath. He didn't know everything. He didn't know what she has seen

"I'm just really curious, I guess," she replied.

She just didn't feel like she should tell him of her visions yet.

Danny took the long way home, and they pulled down a back road to steal a little time together. He had to make things right and have that connection back. He wondered what his mom would say if he knew just how involved they were. They couldn't get enough of each other after the first time.

They were flushed and sweating when a car went past.

"Oh my goodness! Who was that?" Evey shrieked.

"I don't know. No one ever comes down this road unless . . ." Danny trailed off, and Evelyn eyed him.

Then she laughed.

"I guess someone else might need some alone time," she said, grabbing his hand.

They made it home, and Evey filled Grandma and Grandpa in on what all they found out and didn't. She told them that those Indians just didn't seem right. They didn't look like what she had seen in the visions. She also told Grandma that Danny was bored to tears.

"Have you told him yet, dear?" asked Grandma.

"No. I just can't. I just don't feel like I should tell him—at least not yet. Not until I know more. And they think this Daniel Vincent

Bailey is a hero, and I know him to be what he truly is. How do I tell him that?" Evey replied.

Grandma studied her a moment and then said, "You need to tell him soon. If you plan on marrying the boy, he needs to know and accept what is."

Evelyn took a deep breath and nodded.

Grandma took Evey to the neighboring county museum the next day. Grandma loved a good adventure, especially if history was involved. They made it to the museum, and the Karankawa exhibit was front and center. The life-size replicas were breathtaking. It showed a very tall man with blue paint all over him, a pierced lip, and pierced nipples. The was also a small boy with long hair and a loincloth and a woman with a basket. They were fishermen.

These guys look so uncivilized, Evey thought.

She moved along the exhibit to see a number of arrowheads found on a local beach and even what looked like a fishing hook. Then there was the extremely old, black-and-white photo of a young Indian boy, about thirteen. He had on a top hat and suit. Someone had adopted him after his whole tribe had been slaughtered in battle with the local militia, but later, the boy was hung as a thief. They came to find out it may not have been him at all, but no one questioned that a savage would commit theft.

Her heart sank, but that was not her Indian. How would she find her Indian?

Her grandma saw the look of disappointment on her face.

"Let's go ask the ladies here. They may know something else," Grandma said, walking toward the little office, Evey following behind.

"Excuse me, ladies. My granddaughter and I are looking up any information we can find on local Indians, and gwe are actually from a county over. Your museum has such a nice exhibit. Do you happen to know any more information or maybe someone we could call to find out more?" her grandma, asked smiling.

The ladies were all too excited to have someone want to know more. They loved their job, and it showed. They busily pounded on their computer keys to show them the multiple websites that have the most accurate information and what could be trusted. They even printed them a list up of trustworthy sites and gave them their phone numbers if they found something they may need help with.

Evelyn smiled and thanked the ladies.

Not a dead end, just a new place to begin, Evey thought. *I will find you.*

Chapter 16

School and farm life consumed Evelyn, and looking for her Indians was hard. Evey searched online when she had time, but working on the farm and getting her schoolwork done seemed endless. Danny would pick her up in the mornings, and they went to school together. Evelyn was the envy of all the girls. Everyone wanted Danny because of his name and money. Evey just laughed—Danny was hers.

The school days seemed to drag by until, when in history, they got assigned a research paper on local history. This was the perfect opportunity for her to continue her search while getting an assignment done. She was ecstatic. Danny, not so much. He hated writing papers, but she promised to help him. He decided to write his paper on his ancestor, Daniel Vincent Bailey. Evey's stomach ached.

The days went by all the same for the most part—school, chores, homework, supper, research, and little sneak away moments here and there with Danny. Evey seemed to be at a roadblock in her research one evening while sitting at the kitchen table with her laptop out. She looked up to the bar to the blue medicine jar. Dare she hold the arrowhead again?

Maybe there would be something new to see, she convinced herself. *A piece of information to put it all together. I have to try.*

She backed out from the table and walked to the bar and grabbed the bottle. She steadied herself and dumped the arrowhead out of the jar and into her hand. The arrowhead went hot and heavy.

She was running through the woods and heard laughter. She turned to see the strawberry-blonde girl chasing her and in Indian dress. She had a single braid with a pretty white feather. She was catching up.

"Apovini!" she shrieked with giggles.

Evey stopped and turned, and the little girl caught up.

"Angeni," a boy's voice came from her.

She wondered what they said. It sounded like names. She could see a sweet boy's smile reflected in the girl's golden brown eyes. They were playing in the woods together in their dirty bare feet.

Evelyn felt happy. Then as if a switch flipped, their language was now hears. She understood the foreign tongue all at once.

"Where are we going, Wind that Blows Down?" the girl asked.

"It's a surprise, Spirit Angel. Follow."

The girl followed as Wind that Blows Down led her to a clearing to a little oak tree. Evey squealed with excitement.

"One day, this will grow tall, and when we are old, we will use it for our shade," the body Evey was in said, smiling.

"This is our tree," Spirit Angel said, smiling in return.

Something stirred inside Evey, and she sat the arrowhead gently down. At least she didn't feel the need to expel it this time. She felt a little happier with vision of friendship and running through the woods, and she understood the need and love of a good tree.

"Who are you two?" she questioned out loud.

Evelyn was reinvigorated and ready to resume her search and find material for her research paper for school.

"Two birds with one stone," she whispered.

The lady from the library told her to check the Joutel de La Salle. She found it easy enough online. His expeditions are legendary. She read his account of the local Karankawa:

> The Karankawa men shaved their heads except for
> a patch of hair long enough to be braided on the top of
> their heads. One distinguishing mark of the Karankawa

was a small circle of blue tattooed over each cheekbone. Throughout life each one retained a splendid mouth full of white teeth. Dress was scarce, the men wore breech cloths, the women had knee length skirts with no tops, and the children went naked. Some Karankawa wore deerskin bracelets on the left wrist and the men wore small shells, glass, beads, or small disks of tin, brass, or other metal strapped to their throats.

"Dang, those aren't my Indians! Where are they? Who are they?" Evey said, flustered.

"What, honey?" her grandma asked, coming in the backdoor with her herb basket in hand.

"This research is driving me crazy! On a positive note, I have everything I need to write a research paper on the Karankawa, but I'm not any closer to finding who I see. It seems hopeless," she sighed.

"Nothing is hopeless. So they're not Karankawa. Indians tended to travel, and I'm sure the old farts who killed them didn't ask what kind of Indian they were before doing so. It's quite possible a different tribe was around her too," Grandma stated as she plucked leaves from one of her many clippings.

"So how do I find that out if it seems like they are completely wiped from history? No one at the museum even considers there being any other type here. Where do we go from here?" Evey asked desperately of her grandma.

"Let me think on it, my sweetheart. Don't stress yourself on it. Get your paper done, and then we will worry about the next step. You know I love a good mystery," Grandma said, winking at her.

Evelyn felt reassured that her grandma would help her. She was a smart old lady and not only book smart but life wise.

She continued her research on the Karankawa for her school paper, and the more she did, the more confident she was that her Indians were different. The ones she saw were, first of all, not naked and they had their beautiful black hair in full, unshaved heads with a braid.

Danny asked her if she would help him type out his paper, and she said yes, so he came over notes in hand. Her stomach was hurting by the time he was done glorifying Daniel Vincent Bailey for his heroism, smart business savvy, and giving heart for his community.

"Are you okay, Evey?" Danny asked, seeing that she looked green around the gills.

"Yes, Danny. But have you ever wondered if Daniel was as great as you think?" she asked in return.

He looked at her, shocked.

"He was a great guy. Everyone has passed down stories for generations about him. Why do you ask?"

She looked at him, wondering if she should say anything. But she was tired of hiding what she found. How could she tell him gently?

"Danny. I heard he killed a whole family because they were sick and he didn't want them to spread the illness to the town. The problem is, the family lived out here, not in town," she said.

He looked at her with question in his eyes.

"They lived where?"

"Here, where I live," Evey said, looking down.

"There's no way. He was a great man. And if he killed a family, that would mean it was . . ." he trailed off, looking at Evey with questioning eyes.

"My family. One little girl survived, and she was my great-great-great-great-grandmother. Danny, he set their cabin on fire. A father, mother, and baby died," she said, close to tears.

"That can't be right. You talk about it as if you were there," he said.

Evey just looked him in his eyes and prayed that he could see she was telling the truth.

"I've got to go, Evey," he said, getting up and making his way to the door.

The door slammed behind him, and Grandma walked in.

"Danny's leaving already?" she asked, surprised.

"Yes. I just shattered his world. I couldn't handle hearing him put Daniel Vincent Bailey on a pedestal any longer," Evey said with tears in her eyes.

"Oh, honey," Grandma said, pulling her in for a bear hug. "It'll be okay. Things will work out. Maybe this is good. If his mother is so wicked, it may be best to have some distance."

Danny pulled into the driveway and didn't bother to slow down. He came to a screeching stop and ran inside.

"Mom, Mom! Where are you?" he hollered.

"What in the world is all this fuss about?" she came in from the porch.

"Is it true?" he demanded.

"Is what true, Danny?" she asked, annoyed.

"Did our famous Daniel murder a family?" he yelled.

She looked at him in shock and horror.

"How dare you say such a thing?" she asked him.

"How dare I say such a thing? Mother, you've been trying to get me to marry this girl for her land since I was a child to just move the Baileys up another notch in the world, and today I find out that he set a cabin on fire with an entire family inside but one girl survived. She's the girl you were talking about, isn't she?" he questioned her, face growing red. "Isn't she?"

"Who told you that?" Mrs. Bailey said in between clenched teeth.

"Is it true, Mother?" He asked again.

"Yes. The family was sick, and they would have caused an epidemic. In those days, a fever would kill you. He had to do them in for the greater good," she said.

"The greater good? Really? He wasn't too worried if he walked into the house to set it on fire. It's always about more money or more land, isn't it?" he questioned, his face hot.

"Everything we do is for the future of our family. Who told you that? No one could possibly know," she demanded to know how he found out.

"Evey found out. Our family almost wiped hers out, and now you want me to marry her and stifle her. I won't do it. I'm done," he said turning to storm off.

"You turn and walk out of here, and I'll take everything away from you," his mother threatened. "You will get nothing and have nothing to live on. Mind your tongue when you speak to me. You will marry her and get that land, and that is final. Now go tell her she's wrong and ask her how she came to that conclusion. You can also tell her that we will be going to Colorado for Christmas. A little time apart may do you some good. You need to clear your head and get back to business."

Mrs. Bailey smirked, knowing that her son would do her bidding because he would be too scared to not have the life he was accustomed to.

Danny dialed the farmhouse number with his hands trembling. He wanted so badly to tell her the truth, but he couldn't. He knew his mother would listen in on the other line.

Grandpa answered in his deep voice, and Danny asked to speak with Evey.

"Hello," Evey answered the phone.

"Hey, babe, it's me. I wanted to say sorry about earlier. What you said really shook me, and I asked my mom, and there's just no way that can be true."

Evey's heart sank. She stayed silent as Danny went on.

"Please don't tell that to anyone else. I just can't believe someone I'm related to would do such a thing."

"I didn't want to tell you, Danny, and I didn't want to believe it either, but I saw it."

It came out before she could rein it back in. She felt sick and looked to her grandma on the couch. She had heard it too. She nodded and came and sat by her to give her support.

Thank God for grandma, Evey thought.

"Wait. What? You saw it?" Danny asked.

Evey took a deep breath.

"Danny, I don't where to begin, so I'll begin at the beginning. I have visions when I hold certain things. It started with the arrowhead. That's why I was so adamant about finding the Indians in our area. I saw them when I held it, and I saw them saving a little girl that has my eyes from the burning cabin. I had to know. Then when you and I were together at the camp house"—she cringed when she said it with Grandma sitting next to her—"I held that pocket watch that has the initials *DVB*, and I saw him murder them. They begged for their lives and their kids' lives. He burned a baby, for god's sake, and he set the woman on fire in her bed, and she locked eyes with him as she died. It was the worst thing I've ever seen."

Evey's voice was trembling.

Danny was incredulous.

"So you mean to tell me that you can see stuff when you hold it like a witch or something? That's crazy, Evey. I hope you haven't told anyone that. So you've dreamed this crap up or what?"

"I didn't dream anything up," Evey responded her voice trembling, angry and hurt. "I'm telling you one of the most intimate things about me, and you call me crazy. Believe me or not, Danny, but Daniel killed my family. Explain why there was only one woman left in my family tree. It all adds up. I'm sorry, Danny."

"Evey, I'm sorry. I just can't believe this to be true. I mean, people don't see stuff when they hold things. That's ridiculous. My family is going to Colorado for Christmas. Maybe a break is good for us," he said.

"So are you breaking up with me?" she asked him.

"I don't know," he said. "I need some time to think."

"Fine," was all Evey could say, and she hung up the phone without saying goodbye.

"I'm proud of you for telling the truth, Evey," Grandma said in a soft voice.

"He thinks I'm crazy, and I'm not so sure I'm not. I don't have any real proof of anything. I don't know if we are even still together," Evey said, tears rolling down her cheeks.

"Honey, maybe it's for the best. If he can't accept you for all that you are and believe you, then he won't build you up or be a good partner. I know it's hard. Broken hearts hurt," Grandma said, rubbing her cheek.

"Grandma," Evey said, looking into her grandma's eyes, hoping she would understand.

"I know, baby," Grandma said. "I know."

But Evey wasn't sure if she did. Evey wasn't just mourning over a lost first love but her lost virginity and the lost future she thought she would have.

"I knew that little witch was up to something. Time with the Indians did make her great-ancestor crazy and then, in turn, made all the women in their family crazy. Great healers, they were once called, but I just say it's a bunch of hogwash!" said Mrs. Bailey triumphantly.

"Mom, you've been scheming for me to marry her and get the land, and you call her a witch. I think having visions sounds crazy, but you can't tell me that they're not real. Are we the monsters?" Danny asked.

"I don't ever want to hear you speak like that again. We are realists, and it's a hard life. Only the strong survive," Mrs. Bailey said flatly.

"I guess you didn't think I'd fall in love with her, did you, Mother? I love her, and I don't see myself without her." Danny looked at his mother.

"Ha-ha-ha! You think she is worthy of you still? If you want to marry her and get me that land, fine. But she will be no daughter of mine trying to ruin our family with her crazy visions," Mrs. Bailey laughed out.

"Well, Mother, what do you want?"

"Hmm, we can still make this work. Spend your Christmas breaks apart and then tell her that you've thought about it and you can let it go and you can still be together. Next thing you know, we will have you married, and as soon as her grandparents bite the big one, we can have her deemed mentally unstable and still get the land," his mother schemed.

"I can't be a part of that."

"So you'll let her ruin your family and our chance at building our fortune more?" Mrs. Bailey asked.

Danny looked at his mother. "I'll think about it. You have to understand that I love her, and I don't want her hurt."

His mother just laughed and said, "You'll do what I want because you'll realize I know what's best."

Danny went to his room and sat on his bed. He felt sick and alone. He knew his mother was a hard woman. He loved Evey truly.

Seriously, how could I even say I love her if I'm tricking her with my mother? Danny pondered. *How could I say I love her when I told her she was wrong? How could she ever love me if she knew the truth?*

"What was that about?" asked Grandpa.

"Evey and Danny are taking a break," Grandma spoke for Evey. "He's going to Colorado for Christmas. He's not handling the truth of Evey's visions well."

"Oh, I'm sorry, sister. If he's not man enough to love you anyway, he's not man enough for anyone. You deserve nothing but the best. Plus, I promise to be a whole lot of fun during Christmas break for you." He wiggled his eyebrows at Evey in a vain attempt to make her smile.

Chapter 17

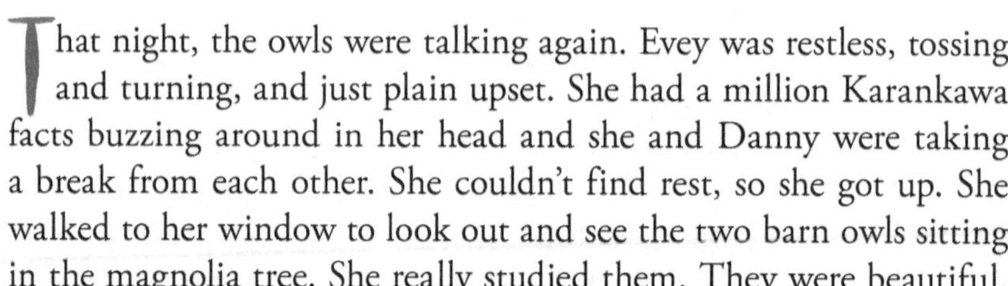

That night, the owls were talking again. Evey was restless, tossing and turning, and just plain upset. She had a million Karankawa facts buzzing around in her head and she and Danny were taking a break from each other. She couldn't find rest, so she got up. She walked to her window to look out and see the two barn owls sitting in the magnolia tree. She really studied them. They were beautiful. She wondered how they came to be harbors of bad news like death. Did that always have to be the case?

Evey opened the window, and they didn't fly off. She looked into their yellow eyes and almost thought she saw a recognition of some sort, but she just shook her head.

"Are you here to tell me bad news or is it something else? You sure have been getting my attention for months now, and no one has passed, thank goodness," she whispered to them, worried to scare them off.

They sat quietly now and just looked at her watching them.

"You are quite beautiful. Maybe you are here to tell me my old self has passed away with the visions I now see. I feel like a completely different person," she said to them, and the wind blew and stirred her hair.

She got a chill, and goosebumps coursed her body.

"Good night," she whispered and shut the window.

The bell rang at the small high school Evey attended, and it was time to be out for Christmas break. Danny walked her to the pickup line at the school, and it was weird. They didn't even hold hands or hardly look at each other. He was leaving in a few hours with his family, so he couldn't take her home, and she was glad he couldn't. She didn't feel comfortable with him and felt like he was judging her. She didn't know how things would ever be the same with them. His mother was mean and didn't like her, and his ancestor killed hers.

Danny had to touch her.

"Let's take this time out to figure out what it is that really want for our future," Danny said, hugging Evey. "I will miss you, and I'm sorry that things are this way."

"I'm not going to change, and I've told you the truth. If you can't accept that, then this break should be permanent."

Evey had tears in her eyes, and Danny did too. She turned from him and didn't look back to watch him walk off.

Danny felt like he was going to shatter, but he felt that's what he deserved for being his mother's pawn for so long. She was surprised to see Grandma driving up. Grandpa always picked her up. Evey raised an eyebrow in inquiry. Grandma just smiled through the windshield.

Evey hopped into the old, blue truck and said, "Fancy to see you pulling up to pick me up."

"Your grandpa was in the middle of something, so I came to get you," Grandma replied, laughing.

"Does he need my help?" she asked quickly.

"No, honey. Nothing serious or dangerous. He is building a few new laying boxes for our girls. And besides, I wanted to pick you up and go for a drink and dessert at the diner."

"That sounds wonderful," said Evey, feeling the disappointment of Danny being gone.

They pulled into the little diner. It was a fifties-style diner like in *Grease*. Evey loved this place. They had the best milkshakes and best pies. They also still did fountain drinks the old-fashioned way.

She and Grandma made their way inside and took their favorite spot, a booth in the corner surrounded by Elvis photos. They ordered a piece of chocolate meringue pie and a Coke to split.

"Thanks, Grandma. I needed this," Evey said as she took a huge bite of pie.

It melted in her mouth like butter on a hot roll.

"I was young once, and I remember," Grandma side, smiling at her.

They finished up their pies and both sighed at the same time and laughed.

"Oh, I almost forgot. I got your Christmas present today," Grandma stated with a gleam in her eye.

"It's not Christmas yet," Evey said.

"But I have to give it to you now," Grandma said, pulling an envelope out of her purse.

As Evelyn opened the envelope, Grandma continued, "I talked to some of my cousins and did some research on my own. Did you know there were actually around fifty different tribes all throughout Texas? Some of the settlements were more permanent. Some of our Indians were Christianized at—"

"La Raza," Evey butted in. "I read about that. These tribes were from farther north, from what I understand."

"Let me finish. So the Indians you have been describing to me sound like traders, not nomads, so we researched where Indians went when they left Texas. A lot went to either Mexico, Oklahoma, or New Mexico. Which brings me to your present," Grandma said, nodding at what Evelyn now held in her hand.

It was two bus tickets to New Mexico.

"So a road trip to see what we can find then?" asked Evey.

"It just so happens there will be a special Indian dance thing going on while we are there. Surely we can find someone who may know something," Grandma said, beaming at Evelyn.

Evelyn felt a new hope surge through her. She was going to do more research and see which Indian tribes were in New Mexico and where ones from Texas may have gone and settled. Maybe her Grandma was on to something, and even if it came up a dead end, it would at least be fun to travel.

"What about Grandpa while we are gone?" Evey asked, worried.

"He and his brother are finally going to go on that fishing trip to the lake, and Uncle's son offered to take care of our animals for us.

It's all sorted out," Grandma said, clasping her hands in front of her on the table, feeling accomplished.

"I can't believe you went through all this trouble. Thank you," Evey said truly heartfelt.

"Well, sweetie, this has everything to do with our family, and I love the mystery of it, and I want you to be able to sleep again," Grandma said.

Sleep—now that's something that would be nice to have undisturbed again, Evey mused.

That evening, Evey sat in front of her laptop, researching the New Mexico tribes. There were a ton of Indians who have moved when unrest hit. How could she find hers? Her heart hurt at the thought that all hers may have been slaughtered. She thought it funny the attachment she felt toward this group of people from the past. How could she possibly call them hers? She looked up the Indian tribes in New Mexico.

"There are twenty-three Indian tribes located in New Mexico— nineteen Pueblos, three Apache, and the Navajo Nation, according to Newmexico.org," she read to herself. "Each tribe is a sovereign nation with its own government, lifeways, traditions, and culture. All welcome visitors, but please make sure to check ahead of your visit as some communities close unexpectedly for religious or other cultural observations."

Her mind swirled with possibilities. She knew a branch of Apaches had migrated to New Mexico. She was saddened when she remembered reading somewhere that before 1900, there were at least fifty different tribes or clans. Texas had a rich Indian history. It was a shame that so much of it was missing now.

The facts she found seemed contradictory to what she knew. The tribes local to her area were not what she saw when she held the arrowhead. The Apaches were not in her area, but that's the only Texas-referenced tribe in New Mexico she could find. There was also the possibility that the tribe went to Mexico.

"So many questions," she said, rubbing her eyes and realizing it was now getting dark.

She carried the laptop to her room. She wanted to just research a little more about the Indian dance they would see. They would be traveling to the mountains of New Mexico to watch the dance of the wind.

She sat down on her bed and opened the laptop back up and put her fingers to the keys, trying to decide what to type or ask, when the owls started talking.

"What do you two want tonight?" she said aloud, feeling crazy about speaking to two birds.

The birds kept on hooting and hooting, so she got up and went to her window to find them on the same branch as always in the big magnolia tree.

"Well, what do you want?" she asked them her golden brown eyes, looking into their yellow eyes.

They weren't like most animals. Most animals wouldn't make eye contact with a human, but these guys were bold. They kept hooting. She just watched for a moment.

"Okay, I'm listening," Evey finally said.

They stopped then.

Freaky, she thought.

One of the owls picked up its wings to show it was grasping something in its talons.

"What do you have there?" Evey asked.

And as if the owl understood, it dropped what it was holding to the ground, and both birds flew off.

Chapter 18

Evey looked at the spot on the ground for a moment then hurried off to get outside to see what the owl had dropped. She wondered if she was nuts. There was no way that owl had dropped something on purpose for her. She went out the back door and around to the side of her house where her room was and made her way to the tree. She bent down under it to pick up a plant.

"That's odd," she said.

She couldn't see well enough in the dark to tell what kind of plant it was, so she walked back into the house and went into the kitchen.

"What are you doing?" Grandma asked.

"It was the weirdest thing, Grandma. The owls were carrying on outside my window, and I got up to see what the fuss was about. When I finally told them, 'Okay, I'm listening,' they stopped, and one of them dropped this on the ground," Evey said, handing the plant to her grandma.

It was a small plant with frayed yellow flowers. Grandma's eyes grew wide.

"What is it?" Evey asked, seeing the shock in her grandma's eyes.

"This plant—I haven't seen it since I was a young child. I'm not sure of its name, but my great-great-grandmother used it in her healings. It's a medicinal plant of some sort. Where on earth did those owls get this?" Grandma said, turning it over in her hands.

"So that plant is an old-school medicinal plant?" Evelyn asked.

"Yes. I think so. I was so young when I last saw this. I wonder if I can get it to grow. I need to find my plant book," Grandma said, making her way into the living room to her bookshelf.

Evey stood in the kitchen a while longer, just thinking, *The owls couldn't have brought me that on purpose. Is that plant important to me somehow?*

"Aha! Found it," Grandma hollered, heading back to the kitchen table with her plant book in hand and the plant setting in the open book.

"It is a fringed puccoon. It says here that the Navajos chewed the roots of the plant for coughs and colds and that word *puccoon* is the Indian word for *dye* because the roots produce a red or purple color," Grandma read aloud, finger following along the page.

Evey thought a little longer and then raced off to her room. Grandma looked up, wondering what just struck her granddaughter.

"Belle Contararo is considered a popular healer among her native peoples in the New Mexico region, including the Navajo," Evey read aloud, typing in, "Woman Indian healer New Mexico Navajo."

"Gotcha," Evey remarked.

Belle had no email address or any claim to any certain tribe, which was weird to Evey. She knew native people were always proud of their heritage, so it seemed odd that Belle didn't have her tribal ties on the web page. But there was a phone number.

She scribbled the phone number down on an old English assignment. She would call this Belle in the morning, her heart jumping with joy. She turned her lights out and rolled over onto her bed, with Tudley at her feet, whispering "Thank you" toward the tree and the owls. She dreamt that night, and she was laughing and happy. It was a nice dream.

Evelyn awoke the next morning to the phone ringing.

"Shoot!" she said, groggy.

It was Danny. She had not figured he would call. The phone was still ringing, and she came out of her stupor.

"Hello," she said.

"Hey, Evey. I just needed to call you. Is that okay?" Danny asked her.

"Oh yes. It feels weird," she replied.

"I'm sorry, it does. Will it always be this way?" he asked, sounding a bit upset.

Evey thought she better tread lightly.

"I hope not, Danny, but a lot has happened, and I don't know if we can be just friends. Did you know Grandma was planning a trip for her and I?" she asked.

"No. I didn't know. Where are you going?" he sounded out, interested.

"New Mexico. She thinks we might be able to find more out about the Indians and have some quality girl time along the way," she filled him in.

"Oh, well, that will be good," he said, trying to sound sincere even though he was upset she was still going on what he thought was a wild goose chase.

Evey heard some chatter in the background. It sounded like they were telling Danny to get off the phone to go skiing.

"Uh, I . . . uh . . ." Danny trailed off.

"It's okay. Go. Have fun," she told him.

He didn't know what to say back. He just said, "Thanks. Same." And they hung up.

Before Evey even hung up with Danny, she was reaching for the crumpled assignment paper on which she had written the healer, Belle's, phone number. Her fingers trembled with excitement as she dialed the numbers.

It barely rang once, and a sweet voice came across the phone's speaker, "Hello."

"Hi. My name is Evelyn, and I found your name on the internet. I've been researching Indians in my area, but I keep hitting dead ends, and I was wondering if you could help point me in the right direction?" Evelyn said.

"Oh sure, Daughter. I would love to help you, but first, tell me which area," she replied, amused.

"Oh my goodness, I feel so dumb. I should've have mentioned that first. I'm from the Texas Gulf Coast. Everything I have found says the Indians in our area were all killed, but I just can't accept that. I need to find the descendants of the local tribe who was once here," Evey said.

There was a pause on the line.

Then Belle spoke slowly and clearly, "Daughter, why do you need to find us?"

"Us?" questioned Evelyn, feeling a spark within herself.

"You were right not to accept that all the Indians in your area were slaughtered. Some made it out, and there are many stories about it. But why is it that you specifically search us out?" Belle asked her.

Evelyn took a deep breath.

Here goes nothing, she thought.

"I live on a hundred-acre farm with my grandparents," Evey started. "The women in my family have always been regarded as healers, not doctors, but healers. And I recently found out that we all have special abilities."

"What did you find, Daughter?" Belle prodded.

"I found an arrowhead, and I just feel like the right thing to do is get it back to its family. I know that sounds crazy, but I don't know how to find them," she said.

"It's not crazy, Daughter. Did it speak to you?" Belle questioned, sounding as though she already knew the answer.

"Well, more like it showed me . . . abilities. Umm, I told you the women in my family have special abilities. When I put the arrowhead in my palm, I saw the boy it belonged to, and when I held it again, I saw more. It scared me, and I threw it down. I was scared to tell my grandparents, but I did, and they've assured me I'm not crazy and have helped me along this journey. I know some of what I see has to do with my ancestors, but I need to find out more," Evey said, hearing the desperation in her own voice.

"I've been waiting for your call, Daughter," Belle said.

"I'm white. I think you should know that. Are you sure you're who I'm searching for?" Evey asked, feeling though she also knew this answer.

"We've been waiting for our Pale Daughter to come back to us, Evelyn. I will explain it to you when you get here," Belle said.

"Wait. How do you know I'm coming to New Mexico?" Evey asked, feeling amused and curious.

"I'm a healer, and the wind speaks to me. I will see you soon," Belle said, and she gave Evey her address.

Evelyn felt elated. She had an address and a name, and she somehow found comfort in the way Belle called her daughter. She thought about being called their Pale Daughter. She wondered what it all meant. She ran in the kitchen to find Grandma cooking breakfast. Chicken and waffles filled the air.

"Grandma, I found our Indians, and all because of you!" she screamed, high-pitched and excited.

"Oh, you did?" Grandma asked equally as excited.

Then Evey filled her in on how the owls dropping the plant and how Grandma finding he Navajo reference helped her decide what to look up—at that point, how it pulled up the name of Belle and how she was expecting her call. She also told Grandma how Belle called her "Daughter" and said she would fill her in when they got there. Evey didn't leave out that Belle had said that the wind speaks to her and she knew she was coming.

Grandma looked enchanted.

"I can't wait to meet her," Grandma said.

"Me either!" said Evey, jumping up and down.

The next morning, they had their bags packed, and Grandpa drove them to the bus stop.

"Take care of my girl and yourself. I love you, sister," he told Evey, hugging her.

Grandpa hugged and kissed Grandma and told her, "Take care of my girl."

He winked at Evey, and she laughed.

"I love you, my sweetheart. Be safe, and you girls have fun," he told, Grandma squeezing her extra tight.

Then they grabbed their bags and got on the bus. It was going to be a sixteen-hour trip across Texas and through parts of New Mexico to make it up into the mountains. The trip was at least eight hundred miles.

Evey could sleep in anything that moved, so she planned to nap along the way. She was too anxious to sleep, and the long nonstop trip seemed to drag on and on. The scenery was beautiful though. The mountains took her breath away. The way they just came up from the ground to meet the sky left her in awe. She had never seen mountains in person before.

The dessert was also unique. She never realized just how many shades of brown there were. Grandma had no trouble napping. In fact, Evey had to nudge her a couple of times for snoring. Evey just laughed. She couldn't believe this once-in-a-lifetime trip she got to go on with her grandma, and she kept replaying the phone call over in her head with Belle.

Then her mind went to Danny. They hadn't talked since the morning she called Belle. She felt a little guilty but was really too occupied with her thoughts. She wouldn't be able to talk to him until she got back, but she was shocked to find she really wasn't too upset. He seemed too busy to talk to her the last time they talked anyway. The quest she was on seemed more important at the moment, and she felt that after she got the arrowhead to its family, life could be normal again. Or would it ever be after seeing so much of the past?

Evelyn was so relieved when they made it to their stop. Hopefully, she could sleep in a real bed. The plan was to settle in, eat, and rest. The next morning, they would head over to Belle's. Evey tried to settle in to the hotel bed. It was comfortable enough, but her mind was thinking of Indians and pale daughters and some of Danny. She wouldn't hear from him for at least two weeks now. She knew he was busy and she would be too, the next day.

"Are you excited, honey?" her grandma asked.

"Very. I hope this is the right people," Evelyn said.

"Everything has a way of working out. Sleep, honey," Grandma told her.

"Yes, ma'am," Evey said, yawning.

When the alarm went off, Evey jumped out of bed and got dressed straight away. She put on a white long-sleeve shirt and cute overalls with colorful patches on the legs. It was December in New Mexico, and it was about fifty degrees. But it was not a wet cold like the Gulf Coast, so she felt fine in her long sleeves and overalls. She brushed her hair and just let it fall wild around her. Grandma put on jeans and a nice sweater and her fire-engine red lipstick, and they were ready to set off to find Belle.

They walked down to the hotel lobby to ask how to get the address that Belle gave them. They came to find out it was only a few blocks away, and they decided to walk. They took in the scenery as they went. It was an old town with a nice square, and as they walked along, the town opened up to what seemed to be even older and they were at an Indian reservation.

Oddly, the reservation claimed no Indian nation name like most. It was surprising how quickly it went from town to reservation. They found the address easily in a quiet neighborhood of similar-looking houses. Evey took a breath and walked through the gate.

Thunk. Thunk. Thunk.

Evelyn knocked on the solid wood door and looked at her grandma, searching for moral support. Grandma squeezed her arm, and all was okay. The door opened, and she was surprised to not see a woman but a young man about her age.

Without thinking, she reached her hand out and set it on the side of his face and looked into his deep brown eyes and said, "I've found you."

He looked a little startled but didn't back away. She searched his eyes and felt home. About that time, an older, gray-and-black-haired woman with deep wrinkles and kind eyes came to the door. She looked to see the two young people staring at each other. Evey's grandma cleared her throat, and Evey snapped back to reality.

"I'm so sorry. I just . . . you look . . ." she stammered.

The old woman smiled.

"Ahh, then we are your people. But we knew that didn't we, Daughter?"

"Yes, I think we did. Belle, this is my grandma, Dottie."

They shook hands and expressed pleasantries to one another for a moment.

"This is my grandson, Anthony," she said, patting his hand and then waving her arm inside to them. "Come in. Come in."

The house was quaint and homey. There were handmade trinkets everywhere, beautiful paintings, and old photos. The inside smelled wonderful like herbs and home-cooked meals. It reminded both ladies of home.

Evey kept staring at the boy. He was so shockingly similar to the boy she saw when she held the arrowhead. She led them in to an old brown and tan couch with some sort of floral print on it. It was really comfortable and well worn.

"So, Daughter, how can I help you?"

"Well, I just need to know what happened at our homeplace. It seems like something bad, but I feel like—actually, I know it has to do with all of us. And seeing Anthony, I know you are my Indians. He looks just like him," Evey said, studying Anthony.

"Who?" Belle asked.

Evey replied without thinking, "Apovini."

Belle's eyes grew wide, and she breathed in deeply. "Who did you say?"

"Apovini. I have his arrowhead—I mean, the one I found is his. I've been seeing through his eyes when I hold it in my palm." She looked at Anthony. "You have his eyes."

Anthony looked at his grandmother.

"It's true. She can see. I didn't really think it was possible, but how else . . ." he trailed off.

"You indeed are our Pale Daughter returned. Perhaps we shall call you Pale Granddaughter. Your ancestor was once our Pale Daughter. Your grandma was right when she told you that there was no way history knew of all the Indians in your area. We, in fact, are a different branch than any you may know about. We've kept it quiet to ensure our safety and peace. We are a secretive people. We hold no claim to any named tribes because we are one of our own. We were a peaceful, trading people. Our name means 'hands of peace,' but we do not breathe it anymore," Belle explained.

"What does Anthony mean about me being able to see?" she asked.

"Well, there is absolutely no way you would have ever known that name without seeing. You know what seeing is, Pale Granddaughter. When you hold the arrowhead, you see," Belle told her.

Evey didn't know why, but she pulled the arrowhead from her pocket and held it out to Anthony. He opened his hand, palm up toward her, and she gently set it in his hand.

"This belongs here with you," Evey told him.

Belle smiled a big smile. She seemed very content with the goings-on.

"Thank you. You really came all this way to get it back to its family?" Anthony replied, looking at her, eyebrows raised.

"Well, yes. It only seems right, and I was hoping to find out more about the women in my family and our abilities. And I need to know what happened to the girl I see," she told him, looking up at him.

"I wish I could see what you do," he said longingly.

"No you don't. It consumes you, and it's scary. You feel alone in the memory, and it feels so real. As long as the vision is nice, it's okay, but the bad ones are hard to shake. I've also held an old pocket watch, and I saw a family die—my family. I saw a woman burned alive in her bed and her eyes—my eyes—looked right at me as she went," Evey said, shuddering and had tears welling up.

Belle sat an herbal tea in front of her.

"Drink. It will calm you. Seeing has its burdens, as does every gift, but you do not have to face it alone. We can help you find out what happened. Come back and have dinner with us. Six o'clock. I'm going to make some preparations, and we will have a meeting by the great fire," Belle told them.

Grandma nodded and told her thanks, and the two of them got up as Anthony walked them to the door and let them out.

Before he shut the door, Evey turned around and said, "I'm sorry I just grabbed your face earlier. It just startled me to see you look so—"

"It's fine," he interrupted. "It's not the first time my handsome looks stopped a girl in her tracks."

He smiled at her.

She laughed and nodded and said, "See you later then."

Evey locked her arm in Grandma's and sighed deeply.

"I like him," Grandma said.

Evey laughed and said, "Grandma!"

"Are you sure these are the right people, sweetie?" Grandma asked.

"I'm positive. Belle knows. And they accept me and the visions," Evelyn said.

"I think this is spectacular to be honest," Grandma said.

They made their way back and explored a few shops in town. They were excited to find an old-fashioned soda shop and got a Coke and a candy bar. At the little shop, Grandma was studying Evey. She looked deep in thought and knew she was worried and anxious to find the answers behind their ancestor. But she could tell there was something else there too—Danny perhaps.

"Are you thinking of what you will find out tonight or about Danny?"

"How do you always know?" Evey looked up frazzled from her thoughts. "Well, Grandma, I was thinking how two complete strangers accept me and my visions just as they are, but Danny won't or can't accept them. I'm not sure if he will ever accept them, and then with our faith . . ."

And as Grandma can do, she finished for her, "You have more questions than answers. I think that faith is something much bigger than we can all imagine, and that bit in the Bible about us not being able to comprehend God's way is a true statement. I don't know why the women in our family can see, heal, dream, know, and do what they do. But I do know that God is bigger than all of that, and why would God not gift his children? Maybe some of us are more in tune than others with the world around us, present and past.

"If it's bothering you a great deal, ask Belle what she thinks and trust that God is bigger than what you could ever possibly know. And as far as Danny goes, he's a sweet boy, but if you have reservations, it's best to deal with them and figure out where your heart stands. A future with someone with whom you can't be your complete self and be 100 percent honest seems like a tough row to ho. You don't have to figure out all the answers at once, honey. I think this trip is a good thing for us both. We get to bond in a new way and you can find out who you really are and what it is that you want in this life. Take this opportunity to explore that and run with it. I love you."

She smiled at her granddaughter, understanding her convictions and worried once again about her and Danny.

Even if Evey were able to get to a point where she could feel comfortable with him, would she ever feel whole with him again?

They finished up their Cokes. They then went back to the hotel to rest. Evey wasn't sure, but she felt like that night was going to be big.

Chapter 19

They were back at Belle's house at six sharp. Before they could knock, Belle was opening the door and ushering them in. It smelled wonderful. She had made beef stew and cornbread. It was delicious. Evey looked around for Anthony, but he wasn't there. She felt a pang of disappointment. Belle was behind her combing her hair.

"We've got to get you ready for meeting. You have beautiful hair, Daughter," Belle told Evey.

Evey smiled at Grandma and said, "Grandma says it's as wild as the wind."

Belle made a deep sound and said, "Of course she does."

"Is everything okay?" Evey asked.

"Yes, Daughter. *Apovini* means 'wind that blows down,' and Anthony's Indian name means 'where the wind blows.' And I can hear the wind. So it just seems fitting that our Pale Daughter comes home and has hair as wild as the wind," Belle explained.

Evelyn and Grandma exchanged stares. So many little things seemed to be connected.

As if Belle knew what Evey was thinking, she said as she combed her hair, "Life to us is like a spiderweb. The web has so many silk lines, and each of them cross at many points and sometimes more than once. It seems as if our web crosses many times."

Evey pondered on all of it as Belle braided her wild hair and added shells to the end of it.

"Do you have anything in your pockets, Daughter? You mustn't have anything on you but your clothes when we go to do you seeing," Belle informed her.

Evey didn't understand why she couldn't have anything else on her. Maybe it would interfere with the vision somehow. Evey reached into her pocket and pulled out a rattler. It was from the snake her grandpa had killed. Belle's eyes grew wide at the sight of it.

"This is all I have on me," Evey said.

"Daughter, I think you are more Indian than you know. Why do you have that on you?" Belle asked her, eyes filled with interest.

Evey looked a little embarrassed at this and just answered, "For luck, I guess? I feel like my grandpa will keep me safe with it on me. He killed it and gave me the rattler a while back."

Belle gave an approving nod. "Take it with you. A little luck never hurt anyone."

Evey nodded and picked it up and rubbed it for a moment and put it back into her pocket. She just couldn't leave home without it, like she was bringing a piece of her grandpa with her.

"Are you ready, Daughter?" Belle asked, looking deep into Evelyn's eyes.

Evelyn nodded, and Grandma squeezed her hand. This seemed like a pivotal moment.

Belle grabbed Evey's hand and led her out of her backdoor and down a little dirt path, past some huge teepees, and to where a big fire was burning and where several elders and sat around it. Anthony looked up at her and nodded to the spot next to him, and Belle took Grandma across the fire to sit beside her.

"Welcome home, Pale Daughter," a really old man spoke up. "We've been waiting for a long time for you to come home. Here you find your family, your people, and, hopefully, the answers you seek. But you must find the answers because we only know stories."

Evelyn was confused. How was she supposed to find answers on her own?

Anthony gently touched her arm.

"I have something for you. The men in our family pass it down to keep it safe until the Pale Daughter returns. And if you can see, you can find the truth you seek by holding it," he said.

"But you are not alone," Belle broke in. "We will send our spirits with you in your sight. That is why we are here in this circle—to support and strengthen you."

Her eyes went back to Anthony as he unbuttoned the top two buttons of his blue shirt and he took something from around his neck.

"This is what I have been charged to protect and keep on me at all times until tonight."

It was a very old leather necklace. It was handmade, and it had leather braided together to look like flowers, and the pendant was a blue stone enveloped in decorative leather. It was very old and beautiful. She took a deep breath, and her eyes widened. She had seen this necklace before. He held it out to her, and fear flickered in her eyes.

"You don't have to do this, honey," Grandma said.

Evey put on her bravest smile.

"I do," she said, holding out her shaking palm up to Anthony.

Evey was shocked when he didn't set it in her hand but instead grabbed her hand with his other and squeezed it.

"You're not alone. I won't let go of your hand," Anthony calmly said.

And while holding her hand firmly in his from the bottom, he used his other to gently place the necklace in her palm and clasped his hands on hers to give her stability and hopefully help her keep the knowledge she didn't travel alone.

In an instant, Evey was brought back to Texas—this time, she was seeing through someone else's eyes. And through the haze of seeing, she heard Belle's voice penetrate her thoughts.

"Daughter, speak to us of what you see, and it won't seem so consuming. Speak."

So Evey did.

"I am looking through eyes of one I do not yet know," Evelyn began. "I am tall and strong with very long hair around my back and shoulders. I'm standing on the edge of a wood, so I have nowhere to seek my reflection. Someone is coming. They are speaking a different language. Strange, but I understand. They are saying *leader* or *chief*. It's a man. He's getting closer. I can see him now. He has on only a leather pants and moccasins and a necklace around his neck with shells and glass on it. He's a brilliant brown from the sun and looks strong. He's saying, 'Leader, come. I see smoke at our friend's wood house.'

"I'm running behind this other man. We come to the other side of the wood to see a clearing with a small wooden cabin. Oh god, I know this place. I've seen it before. I stop quickly and grab the man to get him to stop. There are three other white men, I do not recognize down there, and they are holding torches. One man goes in without even knocking. Oh no. I see a girl running in from somewhere off. I say—or he says, 'Foolish girl. Don't go in. Stay out. Stay hidden. I can tell they mean you harm.'

"Oh no. We can hear shouting, but we don't fully understand English. But we must be friends with the owner of this home. The other Indian looks really upset with the happenings. He says, 'Should we help? He is a friend and always welcomes our trade.' I say, 'No. We cannot. They are armed, and if we go help, even if we are in the right, they will come slaughter our family. We must wait until they leave then run down.' But in my heart, I knew it would be too late. These men meant harm. We hear screaming, and it sounds like begging. Oh no. I know what's happening. I . . ." Evey trails off, feeling the horror of what she knows is happening.

Belle's voice breaks through, "You are not alone. Work through your seeing."

"I hear the most ear-piercing shriek. He's set the bed on fire. I'm in this vision, but I've seen what's happening in the cabin from the watch. A man is trying to get out, but he's kicked back in the house, and they nail a board across the door. Smoke is going everywhere. Leave, you murderous jerks. Leave! I want them to leave so I can see if there is anything to be done. Finally, they leave on their horses. We barely give them time to get out of sight. I'm running as fast as I can down toward the burning cabin. I'm hollering but nothing coherent. I just need to know if anyone is alive.

"Then we hear frantic beating at the door. It's a desperate sound. The door has been nailed shut. We can't get the board off in time. At that moment, I notice the window moving. It is my friend, the man who lives here. He throws the little girl out the window that I just saw running in. She's unconscious. My friend can't make it out of the window. He's too big, sick, burnt, and weak. The other Indian says, 'He will die even if we pull him from here.' I nod and look at him and reach my hand to him. He knows this is the end. I see it in his eyes. He speaks to me in ragged, broken speech, 'Friend, my daughter. Please take care of her. You see what our people did to us because my wife and baby are sick. My daughter. Please. Tell her I love her and'—he broke off, tears streaming—'tell her I love her and to find peace, and please, take her as your daughter,' he said pleading with me. I somehow understand what he's asking of me. I squeeze his hand and nod and look him in the eye and say 'Daughter' in my harsh English.

"He squeezes back with the weak strength of a dying man and falls to the burning floor. It's getting too hot to stand. I focus my attention on the young girl of maybe six. She is the same girl from before. I pick her up gently and start running toward the woods. I say to the Indian next to me, 'Water,' and he takes off, sprinting. Before I get to the woods, a young boy whom I believe to be Apovini comes out with water. He gently takes her head and gives her a drink. I blow on her face, and she sputters and comes to saying, 'Pa, Pa, where are you?' She looks up at me with golden brown eyes and knows.

"She's sobbing, and all I can do is hold her. She buries her face into my chest and is clinging to my hair. I stroke her head. She needs to know she's safe now. I know a few words in her tongue from trading. I say in a quiet but firm voice, 'Okay, Daughter.'

"She looked up then, wiped her eyes, and gave a nod. I squeezed her gently to try to reassure her. I'm thinking, *And they call us savages.* I have strong hands. I sit the little girl down, she seems so frail, but I can tell she's strong. I send the boy off to get someone. Who did I say? I can't quite understand this one. A woman is coming back with Apovini. My mother. She looks so sad at the sight of the girl. She takes the little girl's face into her hands and looks in her eyes, understanding her pain. 'Daughter,' she says and hugs the girl. The little girl hugs her back so tightly that I am shocked."

Evey opened her eyes to see her hands still firmly in Anthony's and everyone around the campfire with their eyes closed, as if they are seeing what she is. Evey is more grounded when she's not alone in her visions.

Belle speaks up without opening her eyes, "Daughter, you are seeing the truth through the chief's eyes. If you can bear it, close your eyes and keep going. You will find what you seek."

Evey notices Anthony's eyes aren't closed—they are fixed on her—and she looks down and notices he has strong hands. Her hands feel comfortable and safe in his. Evey looks him in the eye, and he nods and she nods in return and takes a deep breath and closes her eyes to return to seeing.

"I'm following the woman, she calls me son," Evey began again. "My mother—she is black and white haired with a trim body. She is holding the little girl's hand and leading her back, back home. We come through the woods to find a little village. It's not teepees. It's wooden single-room homes. Longhouses, I think. There are children playing and women outside working and men skinning deer. The little girl is stoic or in shock. Poor thing is almost black from smoke. She's lucky to be alive.

"My mother takes her to a house—our house—and takes her in to clean her. I see a lot of herbs and clay pots. She must be the healer. She cleans the little girl and puts her in a hide shirt until she can make her something more suitable and rubs aloe vera plant and Greenbriar stems on her burns and steeps a bark and lavender into hot water for a tea. She then combs her hair with a wooden comb made from an oak tree limb and braids it back and puts a single feather in the end. 'Daughter,' she says again to the girl.

"The little girl starts to cry, and my mother just holds her in her lap, humming to her and rocking gently. She nods for me to come to her. She pulls the little girl away from her and takes my hand and puts her tiny hand in mine, and she holds one of her hands and squeezes both of our hands and says, 'Family.' She's trying to calm the sweet girl and let her know she's safe, but we don't speak English well.

"I tell my mother what happened and that I gave her father the knowledge that I would care for his daughter as my own in his dying moments. My mother is so saddened by the evil but proud for me to care for this little one. We care for those who are in need. I'm seeing just snaps of time now. It's like a fast forward in my sight," Evey says.

"Tell us what you see, Daughter, it's okay," Belle's voice comes through. "Each sight is different."

Evey feels Anthony squeeze her hand. That little squeeze gives her the strength to go on.

"The little girl is clean and in a hide dress that fits," Evey continues. "She can speak our language now and seems happy. My mother is teaching her the way of the healer. She now knows the uses of the plants in the woods around us. My hand is holding something around my neck. It is the necklace! It was my wife's. She died in childbirth. I lost my wife and child. I never remarried and never had any other kids. I am happy to be Pale Daughter's father. She needs me. She and Apovini have been close since he brought water to her. They play in the woods together often, but he's getting older and will be a hunter soon. Perhaps they should be matched one day. I can see the fondness between them and the cord that ties their spirits together.

"My daughter is running to me from the wood. She has grown and is tan now from being with us. She isn't slowing down. She runs straight to me and jumps into my arms in a bear hug. I smile and ask her what she has learned today, and she says, 'I've learned to fish with my hands and how to sing like the jay.' I smile and tell her I am proud. She does make me proud. She speaks our language well and is teaching us English so that we can be better traders. Our village is prospering.

"Now, I am at a stream. I can finally catch my reflection. I am tall and muscular. I have a scar across my right breast. My eyes are deep set, and I have lines at the corners. My mouth is wide, and I have nice, straight teeth, and my hair is a beautiful jet black with just the hint of silver at my ears. I can see the necklace around my neck. It was my wife's. I made it for her as a wedding gift. There was so much hope for our future, and I loved her so much. Her last words to me were 'You will be a father.' She had seen it. She was a seer. She was right. I am a father. A proud father.

"Some of the tribe was weary of my Pale Daughter not to have been born by my blood, but she was just as much a part of me. Tonight, we would show them. I'm getting ready for something. I'm fixing my hair. It's adorned with many feathers, shells, and a braid.

Lastly, my headdress goes on. I'm going out to a large gathering. My mother and daughter sit together. She is now about twelve by the looks of her and Apovini around fourteen by the looks of him. I give a speech about the prosperity of our people and the importance of family not only by blood but by love and hard work. And I ask for the daughter of my heart to join me in the middle. I say, 'I have called you daughter since the day I picked you up from the ground and you have been mine. Today we all will call you Pale Daughter as you are a part of this tribe, and I give you my blessing.' I take the necklace from around my neck and place it on hers."

Evey paused to breathe. There was so much to take in. She looked around again to see the Indians—her Indians—all softly chanting under their breath. She looked to Anthony to see his eyes still fixed on her. She breathed deeply and continued.

"Now I'm more like me. I'm Pale Daughter. My hands are delicate and worn and stained purple at the fingertips from plants."

Evey felt a pang of realization in her very core when she realized her fingertips were stained from the puccoon plant. Pale Daughter is one with me, she thought, and continued speaking what she was seeing:

"I smell like herbs and am already getting a reputation as a healer like my grandmother," Evey continued. "I brew good bark teas for headaches. With the necklace around my neck, it's a proclamation that I am my father's and I'm recognized as a true member of the tribe. I am filled with pride and a little longing for the family I lost. I will never forget my first parents or the baby. They are a part of me, and sometimes, I feel them around me. Grandmother says I have an eye for spirits. In fact, my pet name from Apovini is Ageni—'Spirit Angel.'

"We are very fond of each other. We grew up together, and he helped me learn the ways of our people and the language. We are growing older. I am now about fifteen and Apovini seventeen. We sneak off alone to our special place—an oak tree that he bent a branch down on to mark it as ours, and it has grown with us. We've been coming her since we were children. We are very close. He knows my every thought, and I swear our heartbeat is the same. It was at this tree when I was ten that he first kissed my cheek, and it was at the tree on my twelfth birthday that he kissed me for real. I remember it well. He had made me a bracelet from a rabbit hide. He had killed the rabbit, and his mother made stew. But he saved a piece of the hide and cut it into strips and made me a braided bracelet. I never took it off. When he told me happy birthday and gave it to me, I was so excited, I jumped up and hugged him. He sat me down, slowly looking at me, and then very slowly bent his head down and kissed my lips.

"I turned red and looked away and he said, 'Spirit Angel, do not look away from me. I wish to look upon your beautiful face, my heart's heart.' And he pulled me closer as I looked into his eyes and kissed me again—but this time, more sincerely and more thoroughly. It was as if the world all around stopped, and it was just us two at our tree. After that, we would sneak away to our tree to kiss anytime we could. Sneaking away from your tribe of wondering eyes was never easy, and I was pretty sure Grandmother knew. She had a way of knowing things.

"We wanted to marry and start a family, but my father had to formally announce Apovini as my man. I had never spoken to my father about this. It just seemed the natural way of things. Other men in the tribe were starting to notice me. I don't know if it is because I'm exotic to them. No matter how tan I get, I am still white. But I'm considered as a member of the tribe and my father's daughter. I have to say that once you are part of the family, that's it—no one ever questions anything again.

"I'm getting to marrying age, and I'm nervous. Grandmother says my father will get me a good match. The only match I can see is Apovini. I smile, just thinking of him. When Apovini and I get back to our village, there is a lot of excitement. There are new white people at the place where I once lived. I wonder how that could be, seeing as it is my family's land, white and brown. My father wants to go meet them. He asks me to go, thinking my presence will help.

"We walk the two miles to get to the clearing from the woods to find a father and son. As soon as they see us, they look frightened, and the older man reaches for his gun. I immediately speak up and say, 'That's not necessary. We mean you no harm. We just wished to meet our new neighbors.'

"They looked at me, confused. 'What are you doing with the savages, Miss?' the man asks. 'Are you held prisoner?'

"My father spoke up then, 'I assure you she is not. She has been my daughter since her parents were murdered by white men in this very place. So, the way I see it, the one's at fault her are you by being on her land.'

"Their eyes got wide at this. 'Your land?' they said in unison and incredulously. 'How can that be? Daniel said the whole family died of illness,' the older man said."

Evey's eyes opened when she heard Daniel. She thought back to the nasty old pocket watch and its initials, *DVB*. She shuddered as she connected the pieces and continued in her sight.

"'Well, we didn't all die,' Grandmother said. 'And my mother and the baby might have been, but that's not what killed them. It was the men from town, and they tried to kill me with them. They locked us all up in the burning house after setting fire to my mother in her bed. It was the tribe who saved me and have cared for me since.' I felt the pang of hurt from my grandmother's words.

"'Then, I guess we have some negotiating to do with you then, Miss,' said the young man, questioning as to what her name was.

"'I am Pale Daughter by my kin, but my Christian name is Sarah,' she told him.

"'Miss Sarah then. My name is James, and so is my father. You may call me Jim. We have moved everything we have to this land, thinking it was vacant. We apologize for the intrusion, but we have no place else to go. May we place call this place home?' the young man asked.

"'Nonsense. We've come to this place fair and square, and by the looks of it, she's just as savage as them,' the father said, looking her up and down in disgust.

"'Sir, the only savages here are the white men who murdered my parents and then lied to you about the state of what happened at this place,' Pale Daughter spoke up in anger, her face going red.

"The young man looked appalled at what his father had said. 'Pa, she's a woman. You mustn't speak to her like that. And if what she said is true, we owe thanks to the Indians for taking such care of her for so long. Miss Sarah, might you come live with us, your own people, and we care for you?' he asked.

"'She is with her people,' her father spoke up. Both men eyed him.

"'And what do you say to this, Miss?' asked the older man in a snarky tone.

"'I say, sir, that I am with my family. I have been with them since age six, and I do not wish to leave their care. As far as you staying on *my* land, I'll let my father decide that,' she said calmly but fiercely.

"'Then, it seems we need to have a word with your father then, Miss,' said the older man. She looked at her father, and he nodded.

"'Go on home. I'll have two men stay with me here. I'll take care of this,' he told her in their tongue. She nodded and looked at the two men one last time in the eye and made her way back to the woods to find home.

"It had been many hours when her father made it back. She and Grandmother were sitting in the longhouse by the fire, hands clasped and singing. Her father looked worn and worried. 'Father,' she said, searching his face.

"'Son of my heart, oh no. No no,' said her grandmother.

"Pale Daughter looked from one to the other, trying to search out answers, but in her gut, she knew something was very wrong."

The words of the past just seemed to flow from Evelyn. The group around the fire, with their eyes closed, hung on her every word—even the ones that seemed fragmented. This was the story of their ancestors told like they had never heard it before. They knew of Pale Daughter and that she would return again, but hearing Evelyn's sight was more intense than anyone would have imagined.

"I am so scared. I'm not sure of what," Evelyn continued in her seeing. "But it's one of those moments that you just know your life is going to be different from now on. 'Father?' I pleaded.

"'Pale Daughter, daughter of my heart, I love you as fiercely as the plants love the rain. I would do anything for you to keep you safe and make sure you live without want.' His eyes showed such sorrow that her heart broke.

"'What is it, Father? Tell me,' I said, trying to look brave.

"'Those men—they said they will go to town and say that we kidnapped you and we were the ones that burnt the house, if we do not let them stay. You know the white people will believe them. They have been driving tribes out for years, but because we are peaceful and good with trading, no one has ever bothered us, until now. It's always for greed, wanting land or skins or water. They want your land and everything around it,' he said, tears coming to his eyes.

"'They will do whatever it takes to have the land and the woods and do not wish to be neighbors. I can't go to battle with them. The militia is in town, and we will be slaughtered like the rest. And because you are alive, the only way they can legally get the land is if you marry one of them and they have proposed that you marry the son, Jim. They say we have to let you marry him and leave, but if we leave and take you, they will say we kidnapped you and have the militia track us down, and you know what will happen. The only way I can protect you and our people is to have you marry him. He seems much nicer than his father. If you marry him, you get your land and ours, and it's important that we always have one of our people on this land. I'll have to leave you to keep you and our people safe.' The tears were rolling down his face now. For an Indian man to cry, it is out of the greatest sorrow.

"Pale Daughter cried out, 'No. Father. No. You can't leave me. I've already been left by my pa, but please no, not you too. I don't want to marry that man I don't know. I don't love him.'

"Father looked at me knowingly and defeated and said, 'My daughter, I know. I know. I would much rather you marry Apovini too. Your hearts beat as one, but the only way to save both of you is to leave you. If Apovini stays, they will kill him, if you say you won't marry, they will kill you and us. Daughter of my heart, oh how I love you. Raising you my daughter is my biggest joy. I want you to live well and live on our land. Use it and teach your daughters and never forget us.' He hugged her so tight that she thought her ribs would break.

"Grandmother stepped in now, crying as well, chanting under her breath, 'Daughter of our hearts, be strengthened to fight the battle not with knife or bow but with spirit and mind. You will live a full life and raise a daughter to be like our women, and you will be reunited in spirit with your true love. Be strong, my daughter. Your life is worth many more than you will ever know, and from your life comes great love.' And she kissed her and sat her hand on her check, letting tears fall to the ground."

Evey could feel her tears wet on her face and someone humming to her and rubbing her back.

"Go on." It was her grandma who stepped in and gave her the strength to continue. "This poor Sarah. How much should one person have to endure?"

Evey went on with shaky breath and was seeing through Sarah's eyes once more.

"It feels like I've been held between Father and Grandmother for a long time," Evey continued. "I finally broke away and all I could say was 'Apovini.' And I ran out of the longhouse to find him. It was still daylight. It is summer, so the days are hot and long. I find him outside his longhouse. He stands up as soon as he sees me.

"'What's wrong Pale Daughter?' he asks.

"I just burst into tears and run into his arms. He strokes my hair and says, 'It'll be okay. Whatever it is, it'll be okay.'

"'But it won't!' I cried. 'It never will.' He looked at me, so worried now.

"Now I am seeing as if I'm a spirit on the wind. I am no longer Sarah but on the outside looking in. It's strange but feels safe," Evey sounded more calm.

"Just tell us what you see, wind spirit," Anthony spoke softly in her ear.

Evey felt a weird pang at being called "wind spirit" and could have sworn she felt his breath on her ear. She nodded and continued with the heartbreaking account.

"They sat on the ground outside his longhouse, aware that their tribespeople were watching but didn't care. It was a small tribe—they would all hear soon enough anyway. She went through the awful details of it all, and they both cried. 'The worst part of it all is, Father knows I love you, and he would have let us marry," Pale Daughter said.

"'How is that the worst part? At least you know he approves of your loving me and me loving you. No matter what happens in this life, my love for you will never end,' Apovini told her.

"She cried even more at that, and he picked her face up and looked into her eyes, trying to be strong for both of them. He wiped her tears and kissed her. He didn't care who saw.

"'Apovini,' she whispered. 'I need you.'

"'I'm here, Spirit Angel. Whatever you need,' he told her, not letting go.

"'I need you,' she told him again.

"He stood up abruptly then, understanding what she meant, held his hand out to her. They walked out of the village together and made their way through the woods to their tree. He kissed her there as if it were the last time, as very well it could be. She pulled him in as tightly as she could.

"'Apovini, please have me,' she told him.

"He looked down at her. 'Are you sure? We are not wed and—'

"She interrupted him, 'You are mine and I am yours, and I want you to have me.' She couldn't tell him she wanted him to have her before anyone else, but she wanted the first time to be with someone she loved with her whole heart.

"He pulled something out of his little pouch he carried on his waist. 'I know our tribe doesn't have much stock in rings, but you told me how your family had wedding rings, and I made you one,' he said, holding a small ring made from bone and carved with flowers and what looked like swirls of wind on it.

"'It's the most beautiful thing I've ever seen,' she said. She held her left hand out, and he slipped the ring on her finger.

"'Now you are my wife,' he said, kissing the ring on her finger.

"She laughed and cried all at once. She kissed him urgently now. She needed him—she wanted him."

Evey's thoughts were getting jumbled with the visions of who she was. She didn't know where she ended and Pale Daughter began. She felt as though she were a mist on the wind. She wasn't wholly there but so a part of it all. It felt so awful to be in the middle of their most intimate and heartbreaking moment.

"They kissed a lot longer, and she let her hands wander to his hair to let his braid out," Evey went on. "She then put her hands down his leather pants to find what she was longing for. He groaned and grabbed her breasts. Then he gently laid her down on the grass in front of the tree—our tree—and he took his time to undress her, trying to memorize every inch of her. Gently and slowly he readied her. He caressed and rubbed until she was moaning and begging him to please come inside her.

"When he finally did, she gasped, and he looked worried. Sarah kissed him and urged him on. The world stopped. It was just their two heartbeats in rhythm to their lovemaking. She opened wider to let him in deeper, and he cried out and only went a few more strokes and was lying heavily on top, and Sarah was crying. That was the first time for them both, and it hurt their hearts to know that they couldn't grow together in that way.

"'How am I to let you go? I love you so much. I can't just move on or forget,' Apovini said, barely getting it out.

"'I am you wife, now and always, and my spirit is yours. No one can take that from you,' Pale Daughter told him and kissed the top of his head as he cried on her chest.

"He looked up and said, 'And my spirit is yours, and even if we can't be together in this life, I will find you in the next and never leave your side again.'

"She tried to smile at him. She wished they were just going to live their life, happy and together. She had wondered what their children would look like with his dark and her light coming together. The ache in her core was enough that she thought she may just die. He rolled off her now and she lay her head on his chest, listening to his heartbeat—her heartbeat. They always beat as one. And then she fell into sleep.

"They woke to the sun peeking through the tree limbs and the morning dew wet on their bodies. Panicked, she jumped up. But Apovini pulled her back to him.

"'It's okay. I'm sure they know where we are. And I'm not ready to lose this moment with you just yet,' he said, placing a firm kiss on her, his eyes swollen with sadness. She lay back on top of him. They were both slippery from the dew, and he was longing for her.

"Pale Daughter could feel his hardness underneath her. She grabbed it and slid it into herself and lowered down on him slowly. She was tender, but this time, she wanted it to last, and she wanted to remember every moment, every feeling—just everything. Sarah started to roll her hips on him, and he arched his back. She moaned and moved faster, and he bit his lip, trying to hold on for her. He leaned up to take her breast in his mouth, and she gasped, throwing her head back and holding his hair in her hands. Sarah moved harder up and down, and suddenly a wave fell upon her, and she was writhing on him as he came inside her.

"She whispered in his ear, 'Forever you are mine.'

"Pale Daughter fell off him, exhausted and thoroughly pleased. But then, reality sunk in. She was to marry a man she didn't even know, to save her people and, in doing so, lose the love of her life, her heartbeat. She sobbed uncontrollably, and he did too. They would have to leave their spot soon.

"Then the two heard shouting. Someone was looking for them both. It sounded urgent. Sarah looked at Apovini, wondering what to do. They hurriedly got dressed, and she looked down at her finger and bracelet. She couldn't have these on when she left. They wanted no trace of Indian. He knew what she was thinking.

"They started digging with their hands and then found sticks and rocks and dug deeper. The ground was hard. Sarah had to have her most precious possessions safe. Finally, the hole was deep enough. Apovini gave her his sack from his waist, and she put her ring, bracelet, and hair feather in it, and he put his feather and necklace in there too. And they covered it up. She pulled him to herself and cried some more, her heart literally breaking at the thought of losing its beat. Pale Daughter's husband would have to let her go, and she him.

"She had forgotten about her father's necklace around her neck. She quickly took it off and put it around Apovini's neck and told him, 'Please keep it safe for me. I'll want it back someday.' He forced a smiled and nodded and kissed her forehead once more."

That's where the vision ended.

Evelyn opened her eyes to realize she was crying with her head on Anthony's chest. His hand still held hers, but now, his other arm wrapped tight around her, and he was cradling her. She didn't know when she had gotten so close to him, touching in a more intimate way than she had been with anyone else. She was shocked to feel such a way.

She looked up to see his tear-streaked face too, and he looked at her with something in his eyes—perhaps understanding of what she was feeling. They seemed to be so close. She could hear the beat of his heart, and it calmed her.

"Are you the beat of my heart?" she asked in his language—or was it hers now?

Anthony just nodded.

He gently pulled the necklace from her hand and slid it over her head and let it fall around her neck. Something jumped inside Evey at the feel of him doing that and the necklace hitting her heart.

"Thank you, beat of my heart," she said in their tongue, and she closed her eyes and felt him catch her weight.

Evey felt like she was floating and very well may have been. The treacherous long vision tired her to the point she couldn't stand, and the tribesmen carried her to Belle's house where they lay her in a bed. She rested but dreamt of the visions she had seen and Anthony's face and the feel of his hand on hers. She felt like she was being pulled by something—or pulled to someone.

Chapter 20

$\mathcal{E}$velyn awoke, startled. She had been dreaming.

"Apovini!" Evey hollered out and sat straight up.

Anthony was by her side in seconds, with Belle and her grandma close behind.

"Honey, are you okay?" her worried grandma asked.

She nodded and just said, "I was dreaming."

She looked around to see she was in a very nice room. It was well kept and had a beautiful painting on the wall opposite of the bed. It was a scene of buffalo at sunset in the mountains.

Anthony followed her gaze.

"Do you like it?" he asked.

She nodded. "I like it very much. It's so beautiful and peaceful. It gives me a sense of peace when I look at it. The colors are magnificent."

He smiled at her. "That's what I was going for when I painted it. I wanted it to bring a sense of peace to my room."

She was surprised. "You painted that? That's amazing. You are so talented. Wait. I'm in your bed? I'm so sorry. Let me get out and go to the couch or something."

"Absolutely not," Belle said with authority. "You are our guest, and you need to rest."

She turned and walked out of the room. Grandma turned and left to head to the bathroom after being startled awake from Evey's scream.

"Anthony, I'm sorry. I . . ." she broke off, turning away from him.

"It's okay. I don't care that you're in my bed," he said.

"It's not that. I mean, I feel bad for stealing your bed, but it's not that. I completely crumbled in your arms earlier. Thank you for supporting me. You holding my hand is all that kept me grounded. But I am sorry for crying all over you and for what I said," she said, searching his dark brown eyes.

"I'm not sorry for it," he said.

"Was my grandma shocked at what I said?" she asked.

He shook his head no. "She couldn't understand you. You were not speaking English anyway, you were speaking our native tongue. And you spoke it very quietly. I'm not sure that anyone else heard."

"Oh, okay. I'm not sure if I know the native tongue or if that's only when I'm seeing. I know I understand it then. You're not sorry?" she asked, her mind going back to the sound of his heart beating.

"No, it was very intense. In that moment, our hearts both beat together. You are special, Pale Granddaughter," he said, smiling at her.

"I did feel a real closeness to you in that moment. Thank you. Maybe your heart really did beat for mine."

Evey felt such a sense of comfort with him. He was holding her hand and rubbing it. It seemed so natural to her now to have her hand in his. They were both smiling at each other.

Belle was just outside in the hall and overheard their conversation and smiled to herself. She could hear the thumping of their hearts carried on the wind when they were outside, and she also heard what Evey had asked him. The wind carried things to her, and no one really knew how much it carried to her. These two didn't know just how connected they were. Belle walked in the room to break the smile the two were sharing.

"I brought this in for you," Belle said, hanging up the old, brown dream catcher with clear and blue beads and white feathers hanging from it. "My grandmother made this one for me when I was young—to catch the bad dreams. It will help you rest. Now go back to sleep. C'mon, Anthony, and let her rest."

She grabbed his arm, and they walked out.

Evelyn wasn't sure if the dream catcher actually worked or if she were just too tired to dream anymore, but she slept.

Evey woke in the morning to sunshine peeking through the window. She rolled over and groaned.

"You okay?" Anthony asked, coming in from the hall.

"Yes, I just feel like I've been hit by a train," she replied.

He smiled at her. "Well, the seeing was super hard on you, and you tossed and turned for a long time last night. Come on, my grandmother is cooking breakfast, and then she's taking you and your grandma to her friend's to get an outfit for tonight."

"An outfit?" she asked, still feeling dazed.

"Tonight is the Indian dance, remember? This one is the private ceremony, and only our kin are allowed. And now you will be coming as one of us," he said, watching her to see her reaction.

"Now this is the way?" she asked in the native tongue.

He shot up his eyebrows in surprise. It was still weird to hear someone not raised among them speak their long-forgotten language; not even other tribes knew their tongue. It was only passed down to those who were born on the reservation.

"You have shown yourself to be one of us, and last night I formally accepted you into the tribe," Anthony replied her in the same language.

She looked confused. She didn't remember being accepted into the tribe. He didn't know if she didn't understand what he said or what happened.

"I understand what you say, but I do not understand how I am one with you," she spoke again in his language to be sure he knew what she meant.

"Ah, okay," Anthony said in English as he took the three or four steps to get to her.

He reached down and grasped the necklace that was now on her neck, and her body went hot with the touch of his hand on her chest where the necklace sat. She was a little disconcerted at how her body reacted to him.

"You were made part of our tribe when I put this around your neck right before we carried you in," he explained, looking directly into her eyes.

It struck him how beautiful Evey's eyes were in the morning light, and a smile crept onto his face. She couldn't help but smile back and felt a sense of security with him so near.

"Just like Sarah's father placing the necklace on her. Thank you, Anthony. Thank you for keeping it safe for me, and thank you for keeping me safe," she said, meaning it with every ounce of her being.

He looked down at her, not sure how he managed to keep her safe but said, "You're welcome."

"Anthony, where are your parents?" Evey asked.

He frowned deeply. She saw the hurt in his eyes. She felt she should tell him of hers first all of a sudden.

"Mine died in a car accident when I was eight years old, and I've lived with my grandparents ever since. I think that's why Pale Daughter's story hits home hard for me. I know what it's like to lose your parents suddenly and all at once," Evey said, searching his face.

Anthony took a deep breath and then said, "I live here, I think you now know, as you are laying in my bed. My dad was killed in a loading accident at work when I was ten. My mom couldn't bear life without him, and she killed herself while I was at school. I came home to find her on the kitchen floor. She poisoned herself with too much foxglove. Your visions bring that up for me, and I know that even though it's just a memory, seeing someone die never truly leaves you. I understand that much, and that's why I have to hold your hand when you see. No one should face that alone, but you did already with the arrowhead. I'm sorry about that. So I've been here ever since, and that's when I took up painting. It calms me and helps me lose the bad memory for a little while."

Evey thought he looked older than he really was.

"I'm sorry, Anthony. You don't have to apologize to me about anything. I wish you wouldn't have had to go through yours alone either. But neither one of us is really alone. We have family," she whispered, reaching out to touch his arm.

He relaxed a bit with her touch and unclenched his jaw. She saw the hurt in him.

Anthony nodded and said, "It's okay now. Go on, my grandmother is waiting."

Evey got dressed, washed her face, and made her way to the kitchen. The food smelled wonderful. She found her grandma and Belle in animated conversation. Her grandma found a kindred spirit in this woman, and they hit it off right away. They discussed everything, from herbs to how dumb modern medicine was, and now were in intense conversation about Evelyn and her current relationship status.

"Evey has been dating this boy named Danny since she was about fifteen, but he's not able to accept her and her visons. They went their separate ways before we left. I think it's for the best. You know how you were speaking of the spiderweb?"

Belle nodded.

"Well, this boy's family is part of it. His ancestor is the one who murdered ours—all but Sarah. It's a shame because he's a sweet boy, but his family is just arrogant and—"

Evey cleared her throat.

"Good morning, ladies."

"Oh, good morning, honey. How are you feeling?" Grandma asked.

"Much better now. Thanks, Grandma," she said, eyeing her.

"Did you sleep more soundly after I brought in the dream catcher, Daughter?" Belle asked.

"Yes, ma'am. I think it really helped. Before I was dreaming of . . ." she trailed off, remembering dreaming of Anthony and Apovini and just about everything. She guessed the past and present got mixed up in her dreams.

"Yes?" Belle questioned, wanting her to go on. "Indians find dreams very telling of one's spirit."

"Oh, it was nothing. My head just must have been mixed up after everything last night. Where's Anthony?" she asked, noticing he wasn't in the kitchen.

Belle raised an eyebrow and shot a glance at her grandma.

"He grabbed a quick breakfast and had to head down to the community center so he could practice with the other young men of the tribe the Dance of the Wind for tonight," she told her.

Evey remembered feeling like a spirit on the wind in her vision and went back to thinking about Belle's spiderweb. Everything really was crossing for her like a spider's web. Evey just nodded and then ate.

Belle had made toast, and there was homemade jam. She also fried eggs and sausage, and they were all good. They finished up their breakfast and went out the door to go to Belle's friend's house.

"Anthony said we are going to get outfits for tonight?" Evey asked as they made their way down the small path.

"Yes, Daughter. You need the proper attire so you may sit with me at the table. You are one of us. Tonight is the formal ceremony for the tribe, so only tribal members are allowed to be present. Tomorrow is open to the public and is more relaxed as we let visitors come in and watch. Anthony told me he told you. He did, right?" Belle asked her.

"Oh, yes, he did. I just didn't realize I would need to be a part of the ceremony. And Grandma too?" Evey added.

"Daughter, all the women in your family have been born as our people but just didn't know. Even we didn't know who you were, and we didn't have any pictures to go on. But by the stories passed down, I think you must look a lot like the Pale Daughter did. Plus, your homecoming is something to celebrate at the ceremony. Our people will be excited to see our stories and prophecies come to life. You have more than proven you are our Pale Daughter who was said would return to us. You see our past and know our tongue. You are tied to us in more ways than you know," Belle said this with a knowing smile on her face.

Evey wondered just what all she meant by that but didn't ask.

They made it to a small two-room home. A small, round woman who looked to be at least one hundred greeted them with a big toothless smile.

"This is my dear friend Analac," Belle said. "She has made all of our tribe's ceremonial clothing for the last fifty years. Analac, this is Evelyn and Dottie."

Both Evelyn and Grandma said in unison, "Nice to meet you."

Analac ushered them in with a wave of her hand.

One of the rooms was a sewing room with many leather clothing items hanging from rods all around the room. There were also tables with all kinds of sewing materials and beads. The beads were gorgeous.

Analac noticed Evey staring across the assortment of beads and asked her, "Pale Granddaughter, do you like the beads?"

"Oh yes. I think they are beautiful. I've always loved turquoise," she said smiling at the little, old lady who in turn smiled back.

You could tell Analac was a wonderful seamstress and took pride in her work. The leather clothing all around the room was breathtaking. There were simple shirts and pants, all the way to big fancy dresses and earrings. The earrings were beautiful, intricate tiny-beaded designs. Evey lightly touched one set of earrings that looked like flowers.

"God has blessed you with much talent," Evey told Analac in their tongue.

The old woman smiled so big, you could see her tonsils with her nonexistent teeth, and Belle was flushed with amusement.

Analac got busy measuring Evey and her grandma. They visited and talked about all kinds of stuff. They found out that Analac had never been married. She just never wanted to. She thought men were too much trouble, and when she said that never being married is why she has lived so long, all the ladies had a good belly laugh. To top it all off, she was in fact almost one hundred! She was ninety-four and still working, had a great mind, and, besides missing her teeth, was healthy.

Analac asked Evey, "Do you have a young man?"

Evey blushed and felt guilty. She hadn't really thought of Danny since her and grandma had spoken about him at the soda shop, and until she had heard her grandma mention him that morning, he hadn't stayed on her mind long.

Maybe Grandma is right, Evey concluded. *The break is for the best.*

"Yes—or, actually, no," Evey responded. "We split before coming here so we can think things through. His name is Danny. I've known him my whole life basically, and we've been together since I was fifteen."

"You're now eighteen. Does he set your soul on fire and he be all that you long for?" Analac asked, raising one eyebrow.

"I've never thought of it in that way," Evey paused.

"If you have to think about it, he doesn't. You don't marry unless you cannot live without them, and I never found one I couldn't live without, and that's why I'm still an unmarried old woman. My grandmother Shine of the Moon told me to marry someone who doesn't set your soul on fire is like to live in a prison," Analac said before Evey could finish her thought.

Analac was very straightforward, and Evey liked that. Belle nodded at this. And to her surprise, her grandma was nodding as well. Evey had seen her grandparents and knew that was the case for them.

"Belle, you were married?" Evey asked.

Belle's eyes filled with moisture as she spoke, "I was married to the most wonderful man. All the men in Apovini's line are loving, kind, honest, and protective men. Their love is their oath. If they claim to love you, not even death can separate their love from you. He was taken from me in the night two years ago. He would have loved to meet you. He was proud of his ancestors and how the strong men came forth from him. He passed the necklace to Anthony on his fifteenth birthday. He was the chief here.

"Pale Daughter's father was chief, and she was to lead this people. But when she had to marry to save us, that left us without a chief to follow her father, and he never had any other children after losing his wife in childbirth. It is said that on his deathbed, Pale Daughter came back to see him, and when he asked her who was to take her place, she said she only had one choice and she chose Apovini a long time ago and that he had borne her mark since she left. That mark was the necklace that you now wear. From then on, a man in Apovini's family has lead our people."

Evey looked at Belle, and she could see her pride and love for her husband. She wanted that too.

Analac rubbed Belle's arm and nodded, and Grandma hugged her.

"Belle, I'm so sorry. I understand what it means to have a good man and love him more than life. I have that in mine. When we lost our daughter, I wouldn't have made it without his love and support or without you, Evey," she said looking at her granddaughter. "I still have him though, and I hate to think of the day he is gone because he is a part of me. Belle, I am sorry."

Belle smiled and said, "I know. I am just lucky enough to have been the woman he chose and to have had what time we had together. We were sweethearts."

Analac was studying Evey from a stool where she was working on their dresses.

"Is something on your mind Pale Granddaughter?"

Evey looked up, startled.

"I have so much on mind, Analac, that I don't even know what it is that I'm thinking," she said, shaking her head as if to clear a fog.

"Try to tell me, Daughter. I am old and may have some advice, but sometimes it's good to just say what's on your mind and let the thoughts out," Analac told her sincerely.

Evey sighed a deep breath and said okay, and she began to speak her heart.

"I have been thinking about everything that has happened since I found the arrowhead, how I've changed, who I've told, how they reacted, and all the new people that I've met." Evey smiled at Analac and Belle.

"I know I possess this gift for a reason," she went on. "And I keep hearing it called a gift, although it feels like a burden. But I am a Christian, and I just don't know how I feel about seeing and about the Bible, and then there's Danny. Grandma said that my faith is bigger than anything else and that I'm not meant to know all the answers, but I keep wanting to find answers. I told Danny about the visions and he thinks I'm crazy, but it's partly because a man he idolized is not a great man and I told him. I don't know if we will ever be the same, and then you asked me if my soul is on fire and . . . I love him. I really do. I enjoy his company, most of the time, and his touch. But I find myself being okay without him. I know Grandma is aching to be back with Grandpa."

She looked at her grandma who nodded at this statement.

"Am I doing the right thing?" Evey asked in a pleading voice.

Analac nodded and thought for a minute and then took a deep breath in.

"My daughter, you have been thinking a lot. Anyone in your place would be doing the same. Does not your Bible tell you that God gives you gifts?"

Evey looked up, surprised at this.

Analac smiled her toothless grin and went on, "Yes, Daughter, I have read the Bible. People my age have had plenty of time to do a lot of things. Why would you think your God and mine aren't one in the same? They are. And did not all the saints have different abilities and qualities? I think you just need to live and learn and be open to the possibilities and what there is to come."

Those words put Evey somewhat at ease.

"But Danny?" she asked, raising her eyebrows.

Analac laughed at this and said, winking at her, "My advice on men may not be as good. As I told you, I never found one I couldn't live without, but that doesn't mean I was a nun either."

All the ladies laughed, and Belle said, "Analac, you devil!"

"Your grandma is right on him, I think, Daughter," Analac continued. "If you don't feel comfortable enough to live in your whole truth, he's not right for your soul. You can't live in a half truth. You will never be at peace. You have time, Daughter. I think you will find soon what it is that sets your soul on fire. It may not even be a man. Mine is making things like dresses and jewelry with my hands. Don't be closed-minded to that, but I have a feeling you may already know what you are burning for, and it's okay for it or he to be something different than what you thought."

Evey sighed heavily. Analac was right, but it didn't make her situation any easier.

"Thank you, Analac. I will remember what you told me."

"Done," Analac said, looking up from her beading table and clapping her hands together.

"Come, Daughter. Let's put it on you," Belle said to Evey.

The skin dress was incredibly breathtaking, and Analac had taken the time to put a little beading on it at the bottom. It was a one-shoulder dress. The stunning Indian dress had fringe at the bottom and was form fitting. It cut down pretty low\ so that you could see the necklace hanging down around Evey's neck. Analac made sure the necklace would be visible. It was important that their people see Anthony's proclamation that Evey was their returned Pale Daughter.

Analac whistled when she saw Evey walk out in it.

"You look good," she said, nodding in approval.

Evey felt good in it. They also gave her some earrings to wear that Analac made to match, and Belle started working on her hair. She braided a single section back by her left ear and fastened it with a piece of leather at the bottom.

"Now what kind of feather should we put?" Belle asked Analac, looking toward her.

"Owl," Evey busted in with her answer firmly in the native tongue.

Both Indian women looked at her shocked, and Grandma said, "English please."

"Owl," Evey said in English so her grandma would know.

"Well, I was worried more about what color as to what type, but why do you want owl?" asked Belle, looking at Evey inquisitively.

"Owls are what brought me to you. I have a pair of owls that talk to me at night. I was upset at first because we've always been told that owls foretell of death. So I wondered why they were coming to tell me about someone dying. But that's not what they were doing— or, at least, I don't think so now—although I do feel like my old self has died away. Maybe they were coming to guide my own self-transformation. Anyway, they have become a normal part of my life," Evey started.

"A pair?" Belle asked.

"Yes, a male and female. They are always together. I never see the one without the other. I felt like they were following me. They haven't left me since finding the arrowhead. I talk to them at night. I know that sounds silly, but I've always talked to animals. Sometimes I think they answer. Anyhow, I've been searching for months to find who the arrowhead belongs to and kept hitting dead end after dead end. I've held the arrowhead several times to try to learn more."

"You held it more than once on your own?" Belle interrupted.

"Uh, yes. Is that bad?" Evey asked.

"Most people can barely handle it the once on accident, much less choose to hold it again and again on their own without being grounded," Belle explained.

"And being grounded was sitting in the circle around the fire and Anthony holding my hand?" she prodded.

Belle nodded yes and then added, "He didn't have to hold your hand, but I think he felt he needed to, and you obviously needed him."

"He made me feel safe and well grounded," Evey added. "Okay, so to go on, I was coming up empty-handed on all my research, not finding what I needed, and I knew by the way the Indians looked in my visions that the Indians we knew about in our area weren't the right ones. My grandma told me not to give up and that she was sure something could be missing from history and so forth. So Grandma got me and herself bus tickets to New Mexico as my Christmas gift. Then we could come visit the reservation and ask questions and hopefully be put on the right track. I never imagined this would be exactly where I needed to be."

Evey smiled at the women.

"That evening after Grandma gave me the tickets, I started looking up Indians in New Mexico," Evey continued. I wasn't really having much luck but was heartened to know that some Indians from Texas did in fact come here. As I was about to wind down for the night, my owls came. I walked over to my window and asked them what they wanted. They are bold enough to look me in the eye, and one of them dropped something on the ground. I wasn't sure what to think, so I went outside to see what it was, and it ended up being a very old medicinal herb that my grandmother hadn't seen since childhood and no longer grows where we are. Then the idea dawned on me that I should be searching for a healer like the women in my family, and that's when I found you Belle."

The women looked absolutely fascinated.

"It was them," Analac said.

"Who?" asked Evey.

"Apovini and Pale Daughter. They are together now for all eternity in the spirit world. It says that spirits are carried on the winds of the wings of birds. It only makes sense that they would come to you, knowing that you're our daughter. They chose you," Analac said.

Evey felt a shiver go up her spine. The spiderweb was becoming more complete.

"Don't be afraid, Daughter. Just be open to listen. It seems like you do that. Is it only birds that talk to you?" Belle asked.

"Evey has always been a caretaker of animals," Grandma spoke here for Evey. "She has a pet coyote that she raised from a baby."

Both Indian women shared a glance.

"All the women in our family have a sensitive side toward animals and just seem to be okay with them," Grandma Dottie continued.

Both women nodded, pleased.

They did find Evey an owl feather and told her the owl isn't regarded as wise for no reason. Evey felt like there was more they wanted to say but held back.

Evey looked into the mirror. She did in fact look very much like an Indian, just a little more pale.

How fitting, she thought.

Her grandma looked beautiful too. They put her in a long-shirt style, a long-beaded skin necklace, and beaded moccasins. They had asked Evey if she wanted some, but she told them she preferred to go barefoot, and the women laughed and nodded in agreement with her choice. There was no doubt about it—she was an Indian.

Chapter 21

As evening approached, all four women walked to the ceremonial ground. It was cool on the way there as it was a December evening, but the women assured her she would be warm enough as soon as they got to the ceremonial site because of the fires and body heat inside the tents. The ceremonial ground was essentially a pasture where they built a big bonfire, had little fires dotted along the way, and had large tents set up with tables and food. You could hear the drumbeat go on as you approached.

Evey's heart beat faster as they neared. When she could see where they were going, it took her breath away. To see so many tribespeople in complete Indian dress was breathtaking. She thought it was quite beautiful.

Belle and Analac led them to a long table. They had told them, each family sits together for dinner, and that night Evey and Grandma would sit with theirs. All the men were standing behind their seats and would do so until all the women got there and would not sit until every woman had. Evey thought this was quite touching.

As she got closer to the table, she caught sight of Anthony. He was tall and muscular with sun-kissed brown skin, and his strong hands were set on the back of his chair. He had no shirt on and was built so well that Evey caught herself staring at him. His abs were perfectly chiseled, and his pecs were nice and hard, with small, round, dark brown nipples in perfect place. He had on a single strap of leather as a necklace with the arrowhead she had brought tied onto it as a pendant. It looked good on him, and her heart leapt at the sight of something she had carried for so long being in the right place.

Anthony must have felt her stare because he looked up to see her, and she immediately looked up to catch his eyes. He smiled at her, and she couldn't help but return the smile. She took his breath away too. She was tall and lean, and her legs were so long and gorgeous. He noticed her long legs first and shoeless feet. It made him smile to see her barefoot. He knew they would have offered her moccasins. Then he let his eyes travel upward.

Analac had made a beautiful dress, but the figure underneath filled it out well. He hadn't really gotten to see her shape before. She had a nice, proportionate shape and nice breasts filling out the top of her one-shoulder dress. Her collar bones were so beautiful to him, and seeing the necklace just sit in place right above her breast gave him a feeling deep in the pit of his stomach. The necklace was home, and he had placed it there.

All three women with her caught the exchange between them.

"That Anthony sure is a sight for sore eyes, huh, girl?" Analac whistled, elbowing Evey in the ribs.

"Yes he is," Evey resigned, unable to hide she had looked him over.

"Don't worry. You look just as good with your long legs and nice neckline and wild hair, Daughter. He noticed you too," Analac told her.

This somewhat reassured Evey, but she felt embarrassed she was caught looking and felt a tinge of guilt as she thought of Danny.

Finally, everyone got there and they sat. Food was all along the middle of each table, and everyone just grabbed what they wanted. Everything from fish, to chicken, to venison, and every vegetable imaginable were served. It was a feast. Evey was seated across Anthony.

Just freaking perfect, she thought. *Now I could sit across my guilt and have him watch me eat.*

She tried to stare down at her plate and not look at Anthony.

"Are you okay?" Grandma asked her, noticing Evey not saying much.

Grandma was in her element visiting and talking about herbs and Texas.

"I'm fine, Grandma. I just feel bad," Evey said, still looking down.

"Are you sick? What's hurting? I'm sure Belle has something to help," Grandma said so fast, it almost made Evey's head spin.

"Not that kind of bad. I was thinking about—"

"Danny?" Grandma interrupted.

Evey nodded. She looked up to see Anthony staring at her with a look of concern on his face.

Why would he even care if I was feeling bad? Evey wondered. He hardly knew me, yet I feel so calm with him and like she'd known him forever. They spoke easily and freely together, and he accepted her. She smiled at him. Grandma was watching her.

"You are young. You don't have to have everything figured out just yet. Have fun on this trip. And for the record, I agree with Analac. You should be with someone who sets your soul on fire. If that's not Danny, that's okay. Better to find out now than ten years from now and two kids later. There's so much more in the world than just what is on our farm, and I think you're realizing that on this trip. Honey, I want you to love someone as much as I love your grandpa, and I want someone to love you more than life itself like your grandpa loves me. Danny is a good boy, but if he can't accept all of you, then he deserves none of you. If you can't feel safe with him, maybe this trip is a great time to think everything through and maybe check out other possibilities."

Grandma put an arm around Evey and squeezed her tight.

"Thank you, Grandma. I love you," Evey said, squeezing her arm.

Evey finished her meal to look up from time to time to see Anthony studying her. She wondered what he was thinking.

Should I ask him later? she thought as she also kept getting that crawling feeling one gets when someone is starring at you.

Indeed someone was. An Indian girl named Lola, and she noticed the tension between Evey and Anthony. She was pretty girl. She was normal pretty though. Nothing too significant. She was shorter than Evey with jet-black hair and a small button nose and a nice smile.

Evey decided to get up and walk around. She told her grandma who was still visiting that she was going to stretch her legs. Evey started walking with nowhere particular to go. She didn't want to go too far and miss the dance.

From time to time, tribespeople would welcome her home or ask her about herself and her visions. Everyone was welcoming and just accepted her. Their eyes all glowed with excitement as the prophecy was fulfilled. Their Pale Daughter had returned home.

As she made her way around the bonfire area, Lola walked up to her.

"Hi. I'm Lola, Pounces like Cat," the shorter Indian girl said.

Evey was a little taken aback. It was different to hear the Indian names.

"Oh, hi. I'm Evelyn, Pale Granddaughter," she replied.

"So it's true then? I had heard there was a meeting the other night to decide if you were really her. I guess so, if you're here," Lola said, examining Evey.

"Yes. It has been a crazy experience for sure. I had no clue until recently and to find out you and your family are so much more than you knew," Evey said to her.

Lola all but jumped out of her skin when she saw the necklace hanging on her neck.

"Who gave you that necklace?" she demanded.

Evey was a little taken aback by her tone. She decided to use Anthony's Indian name when she answered her.

"Where the Wind Blows put it on my neck," Evey said. "It was once my many-times-back great-grandmother's, and now it's returned to me."

Lola looked at her incredulously.

"Anthony put it on your neck?" she asked.

"Yes," Evey just matter-of-factly said, not really understanding why Lola seemed so upset.

Lola had tears in her eyes.

"Are you okay, Lola?" Evey asked her.

"No," she said and stormed off.

"That was weird," Evey said to herself.

Evelyn looked back toward the table to see Grandma laughing and carrying on with the two ladies they now considered friends. They seemed like long-lost buddies. I guess in a way they were. They were such kindred spirits. It would be sad to leave them. They would have to come visit.

By that time, the drums started playing again, and a line of young men streamed out into the middle in front of the bonfire. One of them was Anthony. Belle, Analac, and Grandma all walked around the table so they could see better. Evey was out in front of the dancers, standing alone. She stepped back some to be sure she was out of the way and was excited to see the dance. Some of the tribe made way for Evey to stand in between them.

"Here, Pale Daughter, stand with us to watch your first Indian dance. The one they do tomorrow will be different. This one is special just for us."

She waited until a loud Indian scream shook her to the core, and the men started to dance. She was mesmerized. They were swirling about and stomping and yet so graceful. Their hair swirled around them in colorful fashion with their feathers and beads. Their every move was just perfect to where they only had inches between them.

Anthony caught her eye and wiggled his eyebrows at her. She let out a giggle, and she thought of her grandpa. He always wiggled his eyebrows at her, and she couldn't wait to see him and tell him everything.

Evey's eyes were now back on Anthony, watching his every move and every twitch of his muscles. She noticed he had a nice back. It was muscular and strong. She'd never noticed anyone's back before. She shook her head. Lola also noticed Anthony and saw Evey watching him.

The dance ended, and everyone burst in whoops and applause. Now it was everyone's turn to dance. Lola hurried out to the dance area and swooped Anthony up. She had him by the hands and was dancing really close to him.

Oh, that's why she was so defensive earlier, Evey said to herself.

She guessed that she was his girlfriend. Evey felt silly for feeling a pang of jealousy. After all, she had no claim to Anthony.

Evey walked back to the table to be with the older ladies. Belle was looking at Anthony dance with Lola.

"I've never liked that girl," she said nodding her head in that direction.

"No?" Grandma asked.

"Nope. She's too possessive of him and free with herself," Belle explained.

"She doesn't complement him well at all," Analac chimed in. "Pale Granddaughter, you should go out there and steal him away."

"Oh, I better not. Someone may get the wrong idea, and I don't have a say in who he dances with or likes," Evey said.

Grandma squeezed her arm.

Next, it was time for the Dance of the Maidens. All women who were not married and of a certain age had to go out to the dance area. The maidens were to line up and the single men would march in opposite, and they would dance together as if courting.

Belle and Analac told Evey she must take part, as part of the tribe. Evey noticed there was no age limit for the men. Lola lined up next to Evey.

"Who are you hoping to get as a partner, Pale Granddaughter?" Lola asked.

"I don't really know many of the men here, so I'd be glad to dance with anyone," Evey replied.

"You can't be that good," Lola snorted. "We all at least want somebody cute."

"Cute would be nice," Evey laughed as the music started.

The men started to methodically get in line. She wondered if they picked who they danced with or if it was just random. She hoped to get it over with soon.

"Whoever picks you to dance with tonight, you will dance with tomorrow at the open to the public event," Lola said.

"You mean I have to do this again in front of a bunch of people?" Evey gasped.

"Yep," Lola laughed

Finally, the men seemed to be making their way to get ready.

"The most prominent single man picks his partner first," Lola said.

Naturally, Anthony stepped forward. Evey's breath caught in her throat. He walked slowly toward Lola, smiling. Lola was beaming. But he took the extra step over and was standing in front of Evey. The whole crowd erupted in whoops and clapping. They were pleased with his choice.

He smiled and winked at Evey, and she winked back in return. And over by the table were three smiling women. They were happy with his choice too. But Lola was not.

The music started, and Evey was nervous. She had no clue how the dance would go. She had only ever two-stepped and waltzed. The men started dancing toward the women. She looked around, and the women were all standing still.

So far so good, Evey thought, looking up to Anthony who was serious now.

He made his way to her and grabbed her hands and pulled her to him.

"I have no clue what I'm doing," Evey whispered in his ear.

He chuckled and said, "It's okay. I will lead you, and there are no real dance moves to this one—just how you feel."

She looked at him incredulously, and he just laughed.

The music was a pace above slow. Evey would think the music was more rhythmic than anything. They started to move together. He pulled her in close. Her breasts were squished on his chest, and they both let out a breath. He spun with her, their hair flying around about them. She laughed out, and his laugh echoed hers. She didn't know how, but their bodies just seemed to know what to do with each other. Their steps matched perfectly with each other's.

She looked up at him to see him focused on her, and they were laughing and spinning and enjoying the moment. He flung her around, pulled her back to him, and came up to her, swaying with her from behind. Taking her hands, he then placed them up and around his neck; and he ran his hands down her sides to her hips, and flung her back around to face him, and then dipped with her, and spun again. The crowd roared with excitement.

They were really feeling the music and each other. They were dancing all around the fire, not even noticing all the dancing couples around them. It seemed as if it were only them two. At the end, he lifted her up toward the heavens with his hands under her arms and then slowly let her back down, stopping with her face just inches above his. The music ended, and everyone was clapping and hooting and whistling.

Evey and Anthony came out of their trance to realize it was only them on the dance area. Everyone had cleared out, and all eyes were on them.

"The legend is true," Evey heard a woman say.

She wondered just what that meant.

Anthony walked Evey back to their table so they could get a drink. All that dancing had them thirsty and perhaps a little bothered. Their closeness made Evey want more than she should.

"That was some dancing, you two. It seemed like you've been dancing together for years. Your bodies are in tune with each other," Analac said, nudging Anthony this time, which made him sputter water from his nose.

Evey burst out laughing.

Belle laughed and said, "Well, you two did put on quite a show."

"I have no clue what just happened out there," Evey said.

"Your spirit took over, Daughter," Analac said.

"Everyone can dance, so long as they listen and feel the music," Belle said.

"I think she had a good partner," Grandma said, looking from Anthony to her granddaughter, wondering what might really lie between them.

"I had the good partner. She's a natural and fun to dance with," said Anthony.

Evey smiled at him, and he returned it.

"I think I'm going to sit for a bit," Evey said.

The three older ladies were going to go visit, now that the main parts of the evening were over. Belle wanted to introduce Grandma to all her friends. That left Anthony and Evelyn at the long table all but alone, so he moved over to the other side to sit by her.

"So Lola?" Evey asked; she had to know.

"Ex-girlfriend who wants to get back together. She cheated on me," he said without emotion.

"Makes sense now. She got really upset when she saw the necklace around my neck. Why?" Evey asked him, scooting over a little closer to him so she could hear better.

He pinched the top of his nose and exhaled.

"So you've heard our stories about the Pale Daughter. The men in my family were to wear that necklace and keep it safe until the Pale Daughter comes back to get it. It is rumored that the man who puts it around her neck is to marry her and bind our families together in this life."

"Oh, I see," said Evey, her heart about to pound out of her chest.

He grabbed at the necklace around her neck and gently held it in his hand and said, "I never thought I would be the one to place it on anyone's neck. It's been in the family for so long that it almost seemed like a fairytale. I'm glad it was you though. And I don't think we really have to get married, but I can't hide the fact that I'm drawn to you."

She nodded, knowing exactly what he meant.

"I'm damaged goods, ya know?" she asked.

He nodded and said, "Me too."

"Lola said we will have to dance again tomorrow for the visitors?" she asked, feeling horrified.

"Uh, yes. We do. I'm not sure if we can top that though." He said.

"Top that?" She asked.

"Oh yes. We are a little more flamboyant for the visitors," he said.

"Oh, geez," Evey let out in a sigh, making Anthony laugh.

"So how damaged are you, Anthony?" she wondered out loud. "Oh my gosh, I'm sorry. You don't have to answer that."

He studied her for a moment and said, "Okay. I'll tell you, if you tell me about how damaged you are."

"Fair is fair," she said, nodding, and he smiled at her.

"I told you about my parents. The worst thing in the world was seeing my mother the way I did last. I wondered why she wouldn't want to live for me and if I wasn't enough for her. She loved my father more than life itself. She couldn't wait the years it would take to reunite with him in the spirit world. She wasn't strong without him. Truth is, I wasn't enough for her, I guess. They really did love each other," he said, looking down at the ground and feeling sorrow overtake him.

Evey took his face in both her hands and forced him to look her in the eyes.

"You are more than enough," Evey said so calmly yet directly to him. "Love transcends death, and I'm sorry your mom couldn't realize that. Anthony, you are enough, and you are loved, and nothing you did was wrong. You are enough."

He let out a weak smile. "I've never told anyone that. Who am I enough for?"

She looked at him and, in his tongue, said, "Yourself. Maybe me."

He looked at her for a long moment and replied, "Maybe?"

"I have a lot to sort out with myself. I'm a completely different person than I was a year ago. I'm just now taking a break from a longtime boyfriend and coming to grips with myself. Oh goodness, Anthony, my life was planned out a few short months ago, and then I found this," she said, delicately grabbing the arrowhead hanging around his neck and letting her hand rest on his hard chest.

He let out a ragged breath.

"I feel so comfortable with you, and I'm not afraid to tell you anything," Evey said.

"Pale Daughter, we have time to figure it out—together," he said, gripping her hand around his neck on the arrowhead.

Lola then came over and interrupted their moment. Of course she would. They were just getting down to the important stuff. But Evey wasn't sure if she was ready.

What about Danny? Evey thought. *Am I ready to move on so quickly?*

"Don't you think, Pale Granddaughter?" Lola was saying.

"I'm sorry, what? I wasn't paying attention," Evey said, and this seemed to offend Lola.

"I said that tomorrow in front of the visitors, I should dance with Anthony. You know, since we've done this more than once," Lola offered, trying to stick it to Evey.

Evey looked at Anthony to see what his thoughts were.

"Lola, you know how it goes. I will dance again with Pale Granddaughter tomorrow," Anthony spoke up.

Lola was flushed. She wasn't happy. She was trying to sink her hooks back into him.

The night ended with elders telling stories around the fire, and of course, many of them had to do with the Pale Daughter and her return. Evey was glad when it was time to go. She was tired, and her head hurt from all the thoughts swirling around in there.

They made their way back by walking to Belle's. Since the seeing night, Belle had them staying with her. Evey was glad too. She much preferred their breakfast opposed to the intercontinental one at the hotel. Belle and Grandma walked ahead of Anthony and Evey, talking and going over who all they had talked to that night and who did what in the town. As they were getting closer to home, they heard someone walking behind them. It was Lola and another group of girls. She was talking about Evey in their native tongue and called her a man stealer and a white witch.

Evey turned around, glaring.

In their native tongue—her native tongue—she said, "If I am to be a white witch, then I should think you would mind your tongue."

She whirled back around and grabbed Anthony's arm tight and kept walking.

Lola and her friends stood stark still, with their mouths wide open. No one had ever met a white girl who could speak their language. Anthony was laughing under his breath.

"Really?" Evey said to him.

"I was going to turn around to defend your honor, but obviously you have it under control," he said, still laughing.

She hit him in the side, and he let out an "Umph."

Their grandmothers turned around to see what had happened, and they both started laughing hysterically. They couldn't help but to laugh too, even though they had no clue what they were laughing about. They were just happy to see their grandbabies happy.

Chapter 22

Danny looked out of the window in his suite of a room. It was fancy. It had a full kitchen and a seating room and a huge jacuzzi. He wished he could have Evey in that tub, but he had walked away from her. He wasn't sure that he could ever go back to her with everything that had happened.

He shook his head. She was on his mind right now as he sit in the quiet in his massive room all alone. His carnal needs were becoming persistent. It would be easy to find a one-night stand in Colorado, but he didn't want that. He wanted Evey, but he didn't think he could have her. New Mexico was only 406 miles from where he was. He could make it there in about seven hours. Maybe he could talk his cousin into letting him borrow his car tomorrow, and he could go try to patch things up with her. He wasn't so sure he was ready to let her go. Right now, he just really needed her touch.

Danny's mom knocked on the door and came in. She looked at her son sulking in the windowsill.

"Are you truly that upset over Evelyn still? I thought you may have found some cute little girl to play with while we were here," Mrs. Bailey said to him.

"Yes, Mom. I'm really that upset. I wasn't lying to you when I told you I love her, and I miss her terribly. I haven't talked to her in a week now and can't stand it. I have a lot of questions though, and how am I supposed to look her in the eye when I've been trying to get her land for you and I called her crazy?"

Danny buried his head in his hands.

"Son, if you really love her that much, then go get her. You and your cousin can take my rent car. I'll support you in your decision. You just remember who has had your back your whole life later when the time comes for her to get the land," she said.

Danny looked up, shocked.

"I thought you really didn't like her. That she is crazy from all her teachings from her grandma. Mom, if I bring her back, you have to be kind and fair to her," he said.

"You have my word," she said, taking off her original wedding band. "I love you that much. Go find her and ask her to be yours."

"I love you too, Mom," said Danny.

He was ecstatic that his mom would give them a chance and finally recognized his love for her.

The next morning was Christmas Day. Danny was excited to go find his girl on Christmas and present her with a ring. Hopefully, she'd be ready to forgive him and be his wife. He and his cousin Steve loaded up in the car to make the long ride.

Meanwhile, back in the reservation, Belle woke everyone up singing. She was excited to have her home full on Christmas Day. She made the most amazing breakfast. She made pancakes, waffles, bacon, sausage, cranberry sauce, eggs, and eggnog coffee. It was fabulous. Grandma, Evey, Anthony, and Belle all sat at the table together in their pajamas, laughing and enjoying each other. They truly were like family.

They didn't buy Christmas presents; they made theirs. Evey felt bad because she had no idea that Belle would give her the brown dream catcher and she gave her grandma a recipe book. They were both so touched and hugged Belle's neck.

"The best gift you can get is a true thank-you," Belle said. "Seeing your happy smiles is gift enough."

But Evey and Grandma were going to get Belle something later.

Anthony asked Evey to join him in the living room while Grandma called Grandpa, and Belle ran to Analac's to give her a gift.

She made Analac homemade wine. Evey went into the living room and sat on the brown, floral couch with Anthony.

"I made you something," Anthony said. "Don't feel bad, and I hope you don't mind."

She looked puzzled at him. She did feel bad because she wanted to give him something in return but had no clue she would find a whole family here waiting for her.

He handed her a little box. She opened it up. It was a simple leather necklace with her rattler tied on. He had put beautiful wooden beads on either side and secured it. It was beautiful in an odd way.

"Oh, Anthony. I love it. Thank you," she said, really meaning it.

Evey dumped it gently out of the box into her hand and was immediately taken somewhere else—a small workshop—and she saw Anthony's hands carefully tying the leather around the rattler and saying something as he put the beads on either side. Then she saw herself through his eyes. Evelyn saw herself as he spun her while dancing.

She saw herself holding her stomach and laughing after she had hit him in the side. She saw herself as beautiful as he saw her. Evey saw herself held against his chest as she was tremoring and seeing, and she felt herself breathe deeply. She saw his grandmother make a face at him and nod toward Evey. She felt love.

Evey sat it back in the box and took his face in her hands.

"Is that really how you see me?" she asked him.

He smiled and said, "If you saw me thinking you are the most beautiful thing in the world and that I care about you more deeply than I think possible, then yes."

Her heart was ready to beat out of her chest.

She kissed his cheek and looked at him in the eyes and said, "Thank you. Will you put it on me please?"

He took the box from her hands and gently wrapped it around her neck and fastened it in the back. He then let his hands trail to the front of the necklace.

"Now you can wear your luck from your grandpa and my work around your neck and close to your heart," he said.

Evey was smiling inside out, and her heart leapt at his words. She had to touch him. Evey wrapped her arms around his neck and hugged him tight. She didn't want to let go of him, but she heard her grandma hang up the phone, and she slowly let Anthony go.

They looked into each other's eyes, conversation passing between them, without a single word being uttered.

Chapter 23

Their ride went smoothly. Danny and Steve did make it to the reservation on time. They went in as soon as the gates were opened. It was a little chilly outside, but as soon as they got to where the tents and fires were set up, they felt very comfortable.

"There better be some girls here later. All I'm seeing is old women," Steve said.

Danny laughed. He walked the whole place and never saw Evey or her grandma.

Maybe they would be coming later, Danny thought.

He stopped by the only hotel in town, and the front desk wouldn't tell him anything due to confidentiality. Finally, drums started beating to announce the arrival of the head family. Indians came out in full dress and started dancing around a huge fire in the center.

"Holy shit," said Danny.

Steve looked over to his cousin to see what the deal was. Evey was walking out in full Indian dress with the head family and so was her grandma.

"That's Evey," he said, pointing to the tall, pale Indian whose figure showed perfectly in her off-shoulder dress.

"She's kind of exotic, huh?" asked Steve.

Danny's mouth hung open. "I've never seen her like that. I wonder if that's part of some package or something?"

"I don't know. But there sure are some pretty little natives up there," Steve said, a smile coming to his lips.

Danny kept his eyes on Evey. She seemed to talk a lot to the guy seated across the table from her, and her grandma was in animated conversation with two older ladies. It didn't seem like something they paid for in a package. It seemed like Evey and Grandma knew everyone. He didn't like how the Indian guy was looking at Evey, like a panther stalking its prey. He smiled at her a lot too.

She seems comfortable, Danny mused. *Too comfortable.*

It was time for the dancing. The Indian got up to dance.

Thank goodness he's away from Evey, Danny thought, relieved.

The dance was weird to him, just stomping and twirling. He saw one of the older Indian ladies whisper something in Evey's ear, and she laughed and grabbed her arm. Evey knew them for sure.

Then a really old woman came up and spoke in a native language Danny could not understand and then repeated what she said in English, "For today I tell you is a great day of celebration for us. Our Pale Daughter has returned after so many generations and has been accepted back into our tribe."

She waved at someone from the table to come up. It was Evey.

Evey walked up, and the Indian guy came to her side. She looked at him, and he nodded, and Evey spoke in their language.

When did she learn to speak Indian? Danny thought. *She had done that research paper for school, but this is taking it to a whole new level.*

"She says she is honored to be back with her people and thanks God for the privilege," the Indian guy spoke up, and the crowd erupted in applause.

Again, the old woman spoke, "Now it is time for the Dance of the Maidens. It's essentially a lovers' dance."

The Indian women lined up, and one of them was Evey. Danny was in shock.

"The lover's dance. She's lining up for a lovers' dance?" he said, flustered.

"Dude, does your woman have a side dude?" asked Steve.

"No, she wouldn't. But we are not exactly together. For her to have a new guy . . . that would be so fast," he said, feeling worried seeing the smile on her face.

The men started to file out now.

Of course, the Indian that keeps eyeing her is her partner, Danny observed.

The music began with mostly drums.

Maybe it won't be too bad, Danny thinks. *The Indian is smiling and moving closer to Evey. Of course he's taking her by the hands and pulls her into him. Why is she smiling and looks happy? Why is she swaying her hips to the beat? And why is he echoing her body movements?*

Evey's hand now rested on Anthony's face, and his hands were on her hips as they danced in a circle. In a single swift motion, he picked her up and swirled her; and they were spinning as if they were one person. The other dancers fell away, and it was just the two of them out there as they moved like their bodies were meant for each other.

Danny felt like he needed to vomit. He held it back and watched as Evey's and Anthony's hands caressed each another as he picked her up into the air to finish the dance with her just resting in his arms, their noses touching, and lips almost touching.

She's never looked at me that way, he thought, completely dumbfounded.

Evey had never danced anything more than a two-step with him, yet Daniel only realized now he never asked her if she wanted to do anything more. He stood watching her in awe. It was as if Danny did not know her at all.

"Are you sure that's your girl?" Steve asked.

"I'm sure," Danny croaked out.

Danny and his cousin were handsome among the crowd, so it was only natural they were noticed. A group of Indian girls saw them and made their way to talk to them.

"Looks like we have company coming," Steve said. "I like the one on the left."

Danny laughed.

The girls made their way to them.

"We don't get too many handsome pale faces around here," one of them said, smiling.

"Well, my cousin came to find his woman and surprise her," Steve said.

"Oh, pity. You have a girlfriend," another said.

Danny smiled shyly.

"What does she look like? Maybe we can help you find her. A lot of people vacation here," the first girl said.

"Oh, he's found her already," Steve said.

"Oh?" another girl said.

"Yes, the Pale Daughter I believe you called her, and then she was dancing real close with a guy that's not my cousin," Steve told them, sounding so sad and making a puppy dog face to concerned coos.

One girl really brightened at this.

"Oh, you are Pale Daughter's boyfriend?" she said.

Danny nodded, even if it wasn't all the way true.

"My name is Lola. Did you know she was one of us?" she asked.

"I had no clue," he said, studying the pretty girl.

"Huh. Well, she's been too close with my boyfriend, but I guess that's what happens when you find out you have special powers and belong to the chief's family. My boyfriend is in line to be chief," she said.

"Special powers?" Danny questioned, dumbfounded.

"Oh yes. She can see things. The past, for sure. I'm not sure if she can see the future," Lola said, thumping her finger on her chin and enjoying giving him a shock, and all too thrilled to stir up trouble for Evey.

"Damn, son. That's some messed-up shit," said Steve.

Steve was now in between two girls who were petting him.

"I'm just going to go over here to talk with these pretty ladies. You and Lola go figure it out," Steve said, winking at Danny.

"Can you get me to Evelyn?" Danny asked, looking at Lola.

"So that's her white name. I'll see what I can do. Stay here and I'll came back for you when I can get you to her," she told him and hurried off.

Evey and Anthony were still on their high from performing. She loved dancing with him, more than she thought she should.

"Let's go to the side tent and take a break," Anthony said.

There was a small tent to the side for their families to sneak away to, if need be. She nodded and got up and followed him.

They made it to the tent and sat down in two chairs close to and facing each other.

"I have fun dancing with you. Did you hear the crowd when we finished?" Anthony asked.

"I did. It was crazy. I can't believe I danced like that in front of so many people," Evey said with a flush of pink hitting her cheeks.

"You're a natural. I think it really is in your blood," he said, smiling at her.

"I feel like I belong here, like I was meant to be here, if that makes any sense," she said.

"You do belong here. Our family is whole once again," Anthony said, smiling at her.

Her eyes wandered down to the arrowhead around his neck again, and she slowly reached out and held it, her hand lying on his chest. They were looking into each other's eyes with their hearts pounding. Evey couldn't help but be drawn to him.

Anthony started slowly leaning in to get to her. He was getting closer, and Evey started leaning toward him, as if they were moths to a flame.

When they were less than an inch apart, mouths parted, ready to kiss, a boy's voice pierced the air, "Evey!"

Chapter 24

Evey looked up, horrified to see Danny standing in the tent door, his mouth wide open, with Lola grinning like the Cheshire cat behind him. Danny had seen it all—her grabbing his necklace, the way they looked at each other, and the two ever so slowly trying to connect lips. But he got there in time to stop it.

"Danny," Evey said in a low voice.

She looked back to Anthony, seeing the question in his eyes and knowing he saw the terror in hers.

"Oh, there you are, Anthony. I was looking for you," Lola spoke up.

"I'm sure you were, Lola," he said with a tinge of irritation in his voice.

"Maybe we should go so Pale Daughter can talk to her boyfriend. They have a lot to discuss," Lola said with a snarky voice, smiling at Evey.

"He's not my boyfriend anymore. What did you tell him?" Evey asked, anger rising in hers.

"Just the truth," Lola said, grinning at her.

Anthony put a hand on Evey's arm and looked at her.

"Do you want me to go?" he asked.

She looked at Danny and looked up at Anthony, and he saw the rush of emotions in her eyes and knew she couldn't say what she wanted to. When she turned to look back at Danny, he was down on one knee. She gasped, and Lola grinned. Anthony stiffened and stood even taller.

The exchange between Evey and Anthony had left Danny feeling numb. He knew Evey never regarded him in the same way. But there he was—down on one knee. That was his Hail Mary. He didn't know what she would say. They had shared so many firsts together. He prayed his gesture would work.

"Evelyn, Evey, I've had time to think about us this last week. I can't live without you. I'm so sorry for what happened. I need you in my life. My mother gave me her blessing to ask you. See, she even gave me her ring. Please take this ring and say you'll be my wife. I love you," he said, holding the ring out to Evey.

She looked back at Anthony, with a rush of emotions running through—love, anger, curiosity.

"Evey, I don't care what you've done with this Indian. Just say you'll be mine. Please," Danny was begging her.

He wanted her even more now that he saw someone else so near to her.

Evey held out her hand, palm up, to hold the ring. She wanted to know if she could see like she did with the necklaces. Anthony felt like he was going to pass out when he saw her reach her hand toward the ring. Danny looked at her with curiosity, and as he sat the ring in her palm, she reached back to grab Anthony so he could ground her.

Anthony instinctively took her hand and moved in to hold her. Danny's jaw hit the floor when he saw that.

What is she doing? Danny thought.

The ring had its own heartbeat, and Evey was back in Texas at the Bailey house. She was seeing through Mrs. Bailey's eyes.

"Do you wish to tell us what you see?" she heard Anthony speak.

She shook her head no. She wasn't sure what she was about to see.

"Danny, come in here, son. I've got something to show you," she said.

Danny came walking in.

"This is a map of all of our land, and this circled over here is the land we want to acquire. Some of it should have been ours, but sometimes there are unforeseen things."

"Isn't that the Ermis land?" Danny asked.

"Yes it is," she replied.

"They'll never sell. That's their home, and they love it," Danny said.

"Yes, they never will sell, but if you were to marry their granddaughter, we could acquire it," Mrs. Bailey said.

"I don't know about that, Mom. We are friends. I'm not really wanting to marry anytime soon," Danny said.

"It would be good for our family. She is a pretty girl. You could do worse," Mrs. Bailey said with a flat tone.

Then they were bumping forward to present times and she admitted about knowing about the cabin fire. She was calling Evey crazy and bad because of Indian ties.

Evey threw the ring down.

"How dare you even come here and try to put that ring on my finger after what you've done?" She was livid and looked crazed.

Anthony stiffened back up and looked like he could be a warrior.

Danny picked up the ring and stood up.

"Evey, I don't understand. I love you. I want you to be my wife."

"No, you want my land! *My family's land*! So everything between us was a lie?" she questioned him, rage burning in her eyes.

"How did you—what?" Danny questioned, looking at Evey's hand and then the ring.

"I told you the truth, Danny, when I said I could see things. I just saw myself holding your mother's ring," Evey said in a low, angry voice.

"It wasn't all a lie. I swear. I do love you. It's not just about the land for me. It may have started that way, but dammit, Evey, I fell in love with you. I love you. I want you to be my wife," Danny said, sounding terrified.

"You knew my family was murdered, and you still called me crazy. I saw that part too. Your mother told you the truth, and you still treated me like that?" Evey sounded more stern than ever.

"Evey, you didn't even know them. That was the past—we can have a future," he pleaded.

"There is no future for us, and I do know them now. I saw them die, and I saw Sarah be ripped from the only family she knew twice. You don't deserve me," she screamed now.

Anthony tightened his grip on her. She was going to lose it.

"You're going to throw everything away for what, him? From some visions?" Danny asked, getting angry seeing Anthony standing so firm behind her and Evey finding comfort in him.

"I didn't throw anything away, Danny—you did. You had a chance to make things right and didn't. You've lied to me from day one, and the hurt you've caused me can't be undone," she said.

"But. You. Are. Mine," Danny said, raising his voice.

"No, I'm not. I'm Pale Granddaughter, daughter of the first chief, friends to Speaks with Trees, and fire for Where the Wind Blows. And I am the seer of our people, not yours," she said, standing tall and confident.

"Oh, but you *are* mine. I've had all of you more than once. Does that mean nothing to you?" he asked with a snark on his face.

She felt Anthony go still behind her. She was screaming on the inside. That was not how she wanted him to hear she wasn't a virgin. He deserved to hear it from her. She stood still too.

"You are not one of them, Evelyn. Look at yourself. You're whiter than me! You want to sleep with someone else so you know you're not missing out? Go ahead, get it over with, and then come back to me," Danny yelled at her.

Anthony came around her in a flash and punched him hard in the stomach. Danny went down, gasping for air.

Anthony glared at him and said, "You will not speak to her like that. She has given you your answer. Now go. You have hurt her for the last time. GO!"

Lola stormed off, tears streaming down her face. She saw how Anthony was ready to do anything for Evelyn. He wasn't hers, and there was no denying it. He was all in for Evey.

Danny slowly got up, still gasping; and out of nowhere, his cousin Steve came rushing in. He came at Anthony, ready to fight. Anthony reacted as quick as a fox. He pushed Evey out of the way and took the tackle from Steve. Steve was on top of him and started punching him. Anthony kicked him off him but now had a busted lip.

Evey winced at the sight. Now that Anthony was up on his feet, he looked so fierce. Steve lunged at him again, and Anthony slid to the side and punched him on the side of the face. He let out a yelp but turned back around to try again. This time, Anthony hit him in the nose, and a horrible cracking sound rang in the air as blood gushed from his nose; and Steve went down.

But then, Danny tackled Anthony from behind, and they were rolling on the ground. Evey was getting angrier by the moment. First, he comes in like a knight, she finds out he's lying, he insults her, and then he and his cousin unfairly fight the guy of her affections.

Evey's vision went black. She lunged for Danny. She tackled him off Anthony with a true Indian scream.

Everyone was startled, and people came running in to see what was happening.

Being a farm girl had its perks because she was strong. When she punched him in the mouth, he bled. It took Danny a moment to realize it was her who had tackled him and was now beating him. She was taking out generations of anger on him—for her murdered family, the land, playing with her heart, and for being there. He didn't want to hit her back, but he was about to have to. He was becoming a mess of knots.

Anthony grabbed Evey in one motion and said, "Hush now, it's okay, it's okay. He will leave."

She crumpled into him, hiding her face in his strong chest.

Belle, Analac, and Grandma came rushing in.

"What in the world is going on?" Analac demanded, looking from one bloodied face to another.

All the boys were bloody, but Evey only had swollen hands. Analac nodded in approval, and Belle hit her arm.

"Danny, what are you doing here?" asked Grandma.

"I came to find Evey and ask her to marry me, but she was with her Indian," he said though gasps.

Belle looked at Anthony. "Who threw the first punch?"

"I did, Grandmother. He was being disrespectful to Evey. I didn't realize he wasn't here alone, and that guy jumped me. And as I took care of him, Danny jumped on my back, and then Evey jumped on Danny," Anthony explained.

Belle looked at Evey. "Is that true?"

"Yes, ma'am. I held the ring he brought, and I saw what I can't unsee. He's been lying this whole time. All his mother wanted was for me to marry him so they could get our land. Then he knew I was telling the truth and still called me crazy. He also said some other things that I won't repeat," Evey said, looking down.

"Danny, is this true?" Grandma said, full of hurt.

He didn't say anything.

"Of course it's true. I saw it. I don't think he truly believed until I saw, holding that ring," Evey said, starting to tremble.

Belle stepped in. "Danny, you and your friend must leave at once and come to my tent. I will clean you up, and then you will leave this reservation and never come back again, and you will stay away from Evey and her land."

He just looked at her, and then he looked at Evey, and then he and his cousin walked out.

Chapter 25

$\mathcal{E}$vey sat down in the tent a lot longer, tears streaming down her face. So much had just happened, and she had so much to take in. Anthony had just heard she wasn't pure, and they had just beaten the crap out of Danny and Steve. Her hands hurt. She looked at Anthony. He had a busted lip and was holding a napkin on it, and she saw pain in his eyes.

Is that pain because of me? she thought, wishing her tree were there.

She needed a minute to herself. She left and let Analac take care of Anthony.

Evelyn walked aimlessly toward the trees away from the loud gathering. She needed a moment to think and just breathe. Her body was still shaking from the adrenaline. She found a big rock inside a line of trees where one could perfectly see the moon. She thought it was almost like bathing in the sun, except she was moon bathing, and her heart calmed. She heard an owl and looked up to see the pair she knew sitting above her in a tall pine tree.

"You two wouldn't have followed me here now, would you? Did you see what just happened?" she asked, somewhat laughing. "I'm glad to see you. My life is turned upside down, you know?"

"Who are you talking to?" Anthony's voice came from behind her.

"Are you following me?" she asked.

"You answer my question first, and then I'll answer yours," he said ruefully, full of hope that he could cheer her up.

She nodded up the tree toward the owls. "I'm talking to them."

"They didn't fly off when you started speaking?" he asked.

"Obviously not. They followed me here anyway," she said, eyeing him.

"I guess the owls and I are kin," he said.

"So you were following me," she said.

He let out a sigh. "Your grandma told me you would want some air, but I had to find you."

"How did you know where to find me?" she asked.

"This is where I come to be alone. I just had a feeling I would find you in my spot," he said smiling at her, busted lip notwithstanding. "We just met, but I am drawn to you, Pale Granddaughter, and seeing you lain back on my rock with moonlight hitting you and you talking to the owls . . . you're perfect," he said nervously, as he sat beside her on his rock.

"We've got to go!" Evey sat up, bolt right.

"Go where?" he asked.

"Home," she said.

"Texas? Why?" Anthony asked looking at her, question in his eyes.

"My vision. You were talking about your spot right here. I have a spot too that's mine. Only I'm not so sure if it's mine. I just realized talking to you and looking up into the tree that I know the tree from my vision. It's my tree. I have climbed it since I was a child and sat on this limb that I know was made for me. Now I think it was the limb that Apovini tied down, and it's at the perfect ninety-degree angle to lay out on. If it's the right spot, we could dig up what they buried, and I could maybe find out more, and we will know for sure," she said getting up to run and tell Grandma and Belle.

He grabbed her hand and looked into her eyes. "I just told you that I was drawn to you, and I was about to kiss you in the tent. Does that mean anything to you?"

She sat back down by him and took a deep breath.

"I think you know it does. Since I've been here, I've been drawn to you. My skin burns when I touch you, and my heart beats fast. It's like my soul recognizes yours."

He smiled at her.

"That's all I need to know. When I have you, I want all of you—not just body but your mind and soul. Because I'll give you all of me too," Anthony said, kissing her cheek, wincing a little. "Let's go tell our grandmothers that we are going on a road trip and see what we can find. When you are ready, I will set your soul on fire. We have all the time in the world."

She smiled and felt like she was glowing from the inside out.

When they emerged from the trees together, it was as if the whole tribe had turned to stare. Evey felt embarrassed. Anthony didn't say a word so he just grabbed her hand and led her to their family tent.

"You've been crying, Evey," Grandma said as she touched her cheek.

"I'm okay. I just was thinking many things. Danny showing up and learning that he had betrayed me all that time was a huge shock. Then Anthony came to find me, and I realized that my tree is the one from my visions. We all need to go back to Texas," she said.

Evey told Belle all about her tree and how special it was to her, how it had always been her spot, and how she felt such peace there. Belle said that it indeed sounded like a spirit place and she would love to come and asked Anthony if he was coming.

He told her that he had already made that decision and squeezed Evey's hand.

"I won't go through with seeing anything else unless Anthony is there with me," Evey said. "He kept me grounded, and I just need him there."

Belle looked at her, smiled, and said simply, "You do."

Grandma looked at them both and nodded.

"Let's call Grandpa and tell him we are coming home early. Good thing Christmas break is a long one," Grandma said, winking at Evey.

Evey smiled and then looked to Anthony.

"Well, do Indians have a long Christmas break?" she asked.

They laughed.

"Reservation school is a bit different, but we do have a long winter break," Anthony said, laughing.

The next day, they were busy packing and getting ready for the long trip back to Texas. Analac told Belle she would tend her garden and keep an eye out on the house. Evey was sad to say goodbye to Analac. She was very fond of the toothless old woman. Analac kissed her cheek and told her not to be sad and that the birds would carry her spirit to visit her and of course she could back and visit anytime because she is the Pale Granddaughter.

Analac didn't say goodbye last but instead told her, "Daughter, find what sets your soul on fire and don't let go—be it your man or passion. You deserve to live life to fullest."

When she told her that, her eyes wandered to Anthony. He told her he would set her soul on fire if she wanted him to, and she felt a burn in her core. She longed for that, but Danny's tear-streaked face entered her mind.

They got in the car before daylight the next morning. Anthony loaded up all the bags for the ladies. He wouldn't let them lift a finger. He offered to drive, but Belle insisted he sit in the back seat with Evey and looked at Grandma.

Those two are up to something, Evey thought.

Anthony didn't argue and got in the back seat. They sat on either side with the middle seat open.

Evey looked out window, trying to memorize everything about the reservation before they were completely out. She felt at home in the strange place and truly was sad to go.

"Are you okay, Daughter?" Belle asked Evey. "You look sad."

Evey looked up from the window and replied, "I am a little sad. I'm so happy to go home to see my grandpa. I've missed him so much, but I'm sad to leave the reservation. It feels like home to me too—and Analac, I love Analac."

Belle smiled. "She loves you too. We all do. You know you are our family. You can come anytime. I'm excited to see your home. It will be neat to see where our ancestors once lived and where Apovini started out."

Evey smiled. It would be fine, and she would be fine.

Evey must have dozed off because she awoke to the state where you are not actually awake but aware of what's going on around you. She didn't have to open her eyes to realize that she had her head on Anthony's shoulder and felt the weight of his head on hers. She wondered when they had made it close enough to each other to fall asleep together. Her eyes were still closed, and apparently their grandmothers thought they were both still asleep because now they were talking about them.

"Did you look at them, Dottie?" Belle was asking Grandma.

"I did. They weren't even sitting by each other, and then you turn around and there they are asleep and peaceful," Grandma replied.

"I can see the red thread that binds them," Belle said.

"What's the red thread?" asked Grandma.

"American Indians believe in souls being meant for or bound to one another. You are tied to your life partner by an invisible red thread, and you will constantly be pulled in the direction of your soul mate. I can see their thread. You can too, if you look. Like right now. They are just drawn to each other. He has been so protective of her. I knew it after seeing him hold her through her seeing. She seeks him out too. She needs him to feel safe. I see it," Belle said, nodding toward the back seat.

"I do see it," Grandma chimed in now. "Evey feels troubled though. She feels bad about breaking things off with Danny, but Analac's words didn't just touch Evey. They got to me too. I have that love, and I want that for her. I wish I could have seen Anthony gut punch Danny."

Evey tried not to make a sound even though she wanted to laugh. Anthony must have felt her move because he put his hand on her leg and just squeezed it as if to tell her to settle down. His hand on her leg just made her insides burn for him. She wanted him to touch her, but she couldn't dare say that. Instead, she let her hand carefully fall on to his thigh. If she would have to feel the tension of a hand on her leg, so would he. She felt him tense under her hand and buried her face further into his neck. He smelled so good. He wasn't even wearing cologne. It was just him. It struck her odd that she loved just the smell of him.

"The legends say that the man who places the necklace back on the Pale Daughter's neck is to marry her and bind the families together forever in our world and the next," Belle went on talking. "I was almost shocked to see Anthony place it on her neck. I asked him later why he did when he has only known her such a short time. He answered me, 'Grandmother, I have not the words to describe the feelings I had, and it was almost like my hands were not my own, but I had to. I needed to be the one to place the necklace on her.' And he shook his head. I told him just because the prophecy said that doesn't mean he has to get married right away. But there's no denying the bond they have. I almost wouldn't believe it, but I can see it. She sets something alight in him."

Grandma was quiet for a while and then said, "And he in her. I've already warned my husband that he will see something in his granddaughter with this boy that he's never seen before so he can prepare himself. I noticed her feelings for him at the dinner when I saw the way she was looking at him. I just hope she admits it to herself soon. As much as I don't want her to spread her wings and leave me, I want her to find the one who is the wind for her wings."

"You are an Indian indeed, my sister," Belle replied. "The decision is not their own. It was made already. The thread is there. They just have to trust in what is to be."

"Trust in what is to be," echoed in Evey's head the whole way to Texas.

They made a few stops along the way at major landmarks, get gas, and to go to the restroom but really made great time.

Anthony really enjoyed the trip. He had never traveled outside New Mexico. He had to resist the urge to touch Evelyn all the time. He felt like that was crazy. He had never even kissed her but remembered how close they'd come and what he would give to just kiss her. She had major guilt about what she was feeling for Anthony, especially when she had been dating Danny for so long. Her mind was mixed up with guilt, but she was positive she had made the right decision.

At one point in the trip, Anthony was asleep with his head in her lap and Grandma was dozed off on her sweater against the window. She needed to get her thoughts out of her head. Stroking Anthony's head as he slept in her lap, she began to think. She began to question. She wondered if she were good enough for Anthony after already sleeping with Danny. She wondered if that would hinder their bond.

Belle was watching Evey in the rearview mirror.

"What's troubling you, Daughter?" she asked.

"Oh, Belle, I'm just stuck in my own head. A lot has happened in just a few days," Evey replied, looking down at the handsome head in her lap, with a strong jawline and jet-black hair cascading across her legs.

She smiled and stroked his hair.

Belle saw this, smiled, and said, "You know in your heart already."

"I'm sorry, what?" Evey asked.

"I see the way you look and him and the way you did just now. You looked down and smiled from the inside out. I see the glow in you for him," Belle said.

"I can't deny it. I feel so strongly for him, and I think that's what I'm afraid of. I was with Danny for years and never felt the way I do now. It seems so fast. But I do know," Evey said.

The lips of the head that lay on her lap found a smile in the corner of them, and Evey saw that.

"Anthony!" she shrieked.

"What? I'm just lying here asleep," he said, not sounding like someone who has just awoken.

Belle was chuckling.

He rolled onto to his back to look up at her and thought, *God, she is so beautiful.*

He reached his hand up to cup her face and said, "I know too."

She smiled at him, and Belle was smiling from ear to ear. Anthony could see another worry in her eyes, weighing on her. But for now, he would take this moment for what it was.

"Get up, we are home!" Evey said.

Chapter 26

nthony quickly sat up to see they had turned down a narrow dirt road through a gate that had a cattle guard. It was a beautiful piece of land with trees dotted all around, and cows were everywhere in belly-high grass, looking healthy. He saw the little white farmhouse up ahead that sat in the middle of trees. He wondered which tree was hers and looked at Evelyn who was smiling to see her home.

They pulled in and turned the car off, and a short man with salt-and-pepper hair and a huge smile was waiting on the porch. Evey jumped out of the car and ran toward him.

"Grandpa!" she shouted as she wrapped him up in a huge hug. "Oh, I missed you."

"I missed you too, sister," Grandpa said, squeezing her tight.

And then Grandma was there right in the middle of the hug, and Grandpa hollered, "Grandma sandwich!"

They were all laughing.

Anthony looked longingly at them and missed his grandfather. Evey broke free, and her grandparents hugged a little longer and kissed. Evey was grabbing Belle and Anthony and pulling them over to introduce them.

"Grandpa, this is Belle and Anthony," Evey said, making the introduction.

"Nice to meet you both. Thank you for taking care of my girls," he said as he shook their hands.

Bounding in from the pasture was Tudley. He was yipping and excited.

Evey ran toward him and yelled, "Tudley, my boy. Come here!"

He did too and fast. He jumped at her, and then they were both on the ground, rolling and playing. He was licking her all over, and she was laughing and scratching his back.

She got up and said, "I missed you too. Come meet my people."

Anthony and Belle both felt a sense of pride when she said "My people."

Anthony looked and said, "Is that a—"

Grandpa broke in and said, "Yes, a coyote and Evey's baby."

Belle knelt down with her hand out to let Tudley smell her. He smelled her and wagged his tail, so she scratched him between the ears. Next, it was Anthony's turn. Evey watched anxiously. He held his hand out to Tudley. Tudley tilted his head sideways and completely walked past his hand and sat on the ground by Anthony's feet.

"Oh, it's like that, huh?" Evey asked him, and Tudley barked. "Good. I like him too."

"What would have happened if he didn't like me?" Anthony asked.

"Well, you wouldn't get to come within three feet of me," said Evey.

"I'm glad you like me, Tudley," Anthony said, nodding at the coyote.

"Let me help you get your bags. Kids, y'all help me and you ladies go on in and relax for a bit," Grandpa barked.

Everyone did as they were told. Anthony and Evelyn helped Grandpa get the bags and take them in. After three trips, they had it knocked out.

"Mmm, Grandpa, what's that smell?" Evey asked.

"You didn't think I would go on a fishing trip and not catch anything now, did you?" he said, wiggling his eyebrows at her as she giggled. "Dinner is ready for y'all. I didn't want Grandma to have to worry about cooking her first day back, but after today, that's it. I didn't get married to have to cook for myself all the time."

Grandma came in, laughing, "So you had a rough time without me, did you?"

"It was terrible. So. Much. Canned. Chili. And I was cold in my bed without you," he said, going over to kiss her on the forehead.

"Grandpa!" Evey shrieked, and everyone was laughing.

Anthony could see what Evey meant by her grandparents' love. They had fun and really just loved each other.

Could I give her that? he thought, looking at her, and she smiled at him. *I think I could give her that.*

Grandpa's fried fish, french fries, hush puppies, and green beans were delicious. Everyone told him so. Belle was impressed, and Grandma beamed with pride.

Evey showed Belle to her room upstairs. They had a small loft room with a twin-sized bed in the middle. Although the room was small, it had the best view of the farm from the window. Evey helped her get settled. Unfortunately, there wasn't anywhere else for Anthony but the couch.

Evey felt terrible about it and offered him her bed, but he said, "Absolutely not. The couch will be fine."

"Let's go out to my tree," she said. "Belle, Grandma, do you two want to go out to the tree with us to see what we can dig up?" she asked.

Grandma answered and said, "No. We will sit here and rest. You come in as soon as you find something and let us know what it is."

"Will do," Anthony said.

"C'mon, Tudley. Let's go dig for treasure," Evey told her dog, and the three of them went outside.

Anthony was surprised when she led him out of the yard and through a gate to a tree a ways from the house. He had just assumed the tree was close to the house. The air had a nip to it, but it wasn't really that cold. Decembers on the Gulf Coast of Texas are crazy. It's cool in the morning, warm during the day, and cools off again at night. Sometimes it gets really cold, but doesn't last too long. He recognized the tree as soon as he saw the branch. It was a great oak and very old. They branch was indeed at a ninety-degree angle like Evey said.

"You know," he said, "many Indians would tie a branch of a tree down to be able to mark a trail or something important. It looks like this guy just came untied at some point, but the wood was already set into that position and it just continued to grow. It's amazing."

She smiled and said, "I know. This tree is something really special."

"How do you know it's this tree?" he asked.

"Come here," she said.

And they walked around the side of the tree.

Evey stopped and told him, "Lay down with your head at the trunk and look that way. What do you see?"

He did, and he studied what he was looking at.

"I see a line of trees and what looks like a small opening, and is that a deer path?" he asked.

She was excited, and her eyes were bright as the sun.

"Yes it is. It's a little different now than what I saw in my vision. But everything is close to a stream, and there's a stream on the other side of those trees, and in my visions, I always see the little deer track. It just took me a while to realize I was seeing something that I see all the time but just two hundred or so years in the future," she said in a rush.

"Okay, so where do we dig?" he asked.

"If I'm right, which I'm pretty sure I am, we dig close to the trunk under the branch. They buried the little bag next to the tied-down branch. It was a good way from the tree then, but now it's grown a lot."

He nodded and grabbed the shovel.

Anthony was careful as he dug, digging a much bigger circle than he needed to. He didn't want to mess up anything that may be down there. He dug for a few minutes and then hit something that sounded hard and hollow but not like a tree root or anything solid. He looked up at Evey who looked puzzled. She shrugged her shoulders and bent down to see what he had found. She and he both dug with their hands, stopping to smile when their hands would accidently graze each other. Finally, they found it—a little clay pot that was sealed off.

"That's weird. In my vision it was a sack off Apovini's side. Set it in my hands and don't let go of me," Evey said, holding her palms up to hold it.

"Are you sure?" he asked, looking deep into her eyes.

"I need to know if it's hers before we open it, because to open it, we will have to break it," she said looking at the sealed clay pot.

He nodded and grabbed the little pot and slowly set it in her hands.

In an instant, she was back in time. This time, the tree was a little bigger, but nothing like its current size. She was Sarah and was crying. Anthony gave her hands a squeeze to ground her, and Evey snapped out of it enough to tell him what she was seeing.

"I am Sarah and I'm crying. I'm digging to get to my things under my tree. I see the leather pouch. I'm pulling it up, and I empty the contents into my hand. I've got the bone ring, the rabbit skin bracelet, Apovini's necklace, and our feathers. I put the ring on my finger for only a moment and cry some more, and then I straighten up and wipe my face. I'm grabbing the clay pot. I want these things to be preserved more carefully. I don't know if I'll ever see my love again. I put everything back in the sack, and I pull a feather from my waistband. It's my father's. He has died.

"I went to find him when I got a message of his sickness. I'm still married to the young white man, and I have a daughter. He wouldn't let me take her to see her grandfather, and I cursed him. I said he would never have my love, and neither would any of the men in his family have their wives' love, and he slapped my face and told me to go deal with my savages and that when I got back, never to speak of them again. I don't know how I won't speak of them, but no matter what, my daughter will learn the way of the healer.

"I went the long journey. It took a month to get there on horse. When I got there, my people barely recognized me dirty and in civilized clothing, but Apovini did. He came to me and helped me off my horse. I was so exhausted from the treacherous ride. I collapsed into his arms. I awoke in a small house to a woman washing my hair.

"'Welcome home, Pale Daughter,' she said.

"I croaked out, 'Thank you.'

"And then there was a small boy in there looking at me, and I knew as soon as I saw his eyes. He was the son of Apovini. I cried happy tears. The boy asked, 'What is it you cry for?'

"I told him, 'I cry because I'm happy to know you live, small one. What is your name?'

"'It is Whirlwind,' he said back, smiling.

"I smiled at him and then realized the woman washing my hair was his wife. 'I'm sorry,' I said to her.

"'No reason to be sorry, Pale Daughter. You saved us all. Let me get your ready to see your father,' she said to me. I cried again—this time, out of pain.

"'My father,' I whispered.

"I cried, and she smoothed my hair and said, 'Get your tears through now. He needs to see you well and strong.'

"I nodded. She was right. I got dressed in a hide dress and had my feather in my hair and made my way to my father's bed. They were singing. It stopped as soon as I walked in. Apovini was by his side.

"'Father, I'm here. I'm here, and I love you,' I said as I made my way closer.

"He put his hand out to me, and I was right by his side. He opened his eyes and looked at me, and I put his hand to my face with my eyes filling up with tears. I held them back.

"He said, 'I love you too, my daughter. I've been waiting for you. I had to see your beautiful face and big, golden eyes one more time before I go to be with the spirits.'

"'Father, I love you more than all the stars in the sky. I've missed you so much. You have a granddaughter. I named her Hope because she is my hope for this life. She has my eyes,' I tell him.

"He smiled at this and said, 'Hope. I like it, and it gives me joy knowing you are not alone. I have to have a chief for my people, and it was to be you, but you will have to go back to Hope. Who would you have it be?'

"She looked for Apovini to realize he was behind her, his hands on her shoulders supporting her. She told her father, 'I made that choice a long time ago, when I put my necklace you gave me on Apovini's neck. He's the person I love and trust the most.' He squeezed her shoulders.

"'Good, Daughter. That's who I trust too,' her father said, and he grimaced in pain, and her grip tightened on his hand.

"'I won't leave you Father,' she said.

"'I'm afraid I'm going to have to leave you again. I'm sorry, my daughter. I've never wanted to leave you, but I promise this will be the last time I do. And I promise to have my spirit visit you on the wings of birds and that I never really will leave you. My spirit will be with you always. We will be together again one day. Now, my daughter, it's coming. Please sing to me and open the door that I may gaze out on my people and the sky as I go,' he said.

"She did as he said and sang to him his favorite song in their language, and he held her hand until the very end, and his last words were, 'You, my daughter, will be blessed, and your spirit will find happiness, and all your daughters shall be blessed, and you will be reunited with the ones you love again in this world and in the next, even if it takes generations. Having you for my daughter was the best gift in life for me, and I'm proud of you. You lead your daughters well and know my love for you lives on forever.' And he squeezed her hand and let go.

"'Father,' she whispered even though she knew he was gone and put her head down on his chest and wept like a child.

"Apovini held on to her from behind, and he had his head on her back, weeping with her. Finally, she straightened and wiped her face. She took a feather from her father's hair and put it in hers, and then she took another and put it in Apovini's.

"'Now lead your people and lead them well. Stay out of the wars, for you will not win. Stay low and keep them alive. I love you, and I always will,' she told him, kissing him on the mouth and walking out of the house so her father could be prepped for burial.

"The next two days were a blur. She was told condolences from so many people, and the whole tribe grieved tremendously. Her father was a great leader and a good man. The tribe was happy with Apovini as the next chief. He was the right choice. She also heard that over and over. She asked if someone would make her a clay pot to bury special items in, and they did without asking why. After her father was buried, she was ready to leave. This didn't feel like home without him, and Hope was in Texas. Before she left, she walked to the trees and sat on a large rock.

"Apovini found her there, and he came and sat by her.

"'How did you find me?' she asked.

"'Well, this is the spot I come to when I need to get away, and I figured you would come here too,' He said to her.

"She lay her head on his shoulder and breathed out deeply. 'I want so badly to have my soul on fire with you. I ache to be with you, and I miss your touch, and your laugh, and your eyes,' she said, turning to him to look into them.

"'My soul will always burn for you, Spirit Angel. I dream of you often. I miss you too. We will be together in the next life, if not this one. I promise,' he said, pulling her into his arms.

"She crumbled into him. He picked her head up from his chest and kissed her so tenderly and so thoroughly. They were trying to savor every moment. They finally came up for air, and she said to him, 'I want you to love your wife so that your son will know how to love his wife and treat her right. I was happy to see him. Truly. He looks like you. If you love his mother, he will love you for it and teach his sons to love their wives. So that when my daughter's daughter finds your son's son, he will love her the way you love me. They will know who their soul is on fire for from the start, and they will not wonder or have to hide their love.'

"He nodded and said, 'I will. You teach your daughters our ways, how to be a healer, and to search us out so that she can find my son when it's time. And I will still love you until the day I go to be a spirit, and if I shall beat you there, I will wait for you to come find me too.' And he kissed her again, both knowing that would be the last time they ever saw each other."

Evey opened her eyes to feel a wet, tear-stained shirt on her face. Yet again, Anthony was holding her as she was seeing and weeping. He looked down at her and was weeping too. He took the pot from her hands and sat it down on the grass and pulled her to him, and they wept together. They wept for their grandparents who had to part, and they wept for those who were lost. They both were finally cried out and sniffling.

"I bet we are a sight," Anthony said.

"Snotty and tear streaked. Good thing we came alone," she told him.

He nodded and kissed the top of her head, not realizing there were two old women watching them from the kitchen window.

"They are finding their way," Belle said to Dottie.

They regained their composure and wiped their faces.

Evey turned to Anthony and said, "I'm so sorry."

He looked at her, puzzled. "For what?"

"Anthony, I'm not good enough for the chief of our people. You heard Danny back at the reservation. I'm not pure, and all the talk of visions and legends makes me feel unworthy for you. You are so good and strong. You've taken care of me and not asked for anything in return," she said, holding his hands and looking into his eyes.

He chuckled at this.

"So you think I'm a virgin then? Well, I'm not, and you are good enough. You are more than enough. And that's not true."

"What's not true?" she asked.

"I have asked you for something in return—maybe not in words, but I asked. I want you. I want all of you. I want to set your soul on fire, Evey. I want you to give me your soul."

"Then it's yours," she said.

He smiled from the inside out and held her tight.

She relaxed into him and said, "Set me on fire then."

He laughed and kissed her head, and they headed to the house to tell everyone what they found.

Chapter 27

Grandma made cookies. She saw that Anthony and Evey had an intense moment and could use them. They all ate cookies and had milk at the kitchen table, and Evey and Anthony filled them in about the pot. There was not a dry eye at the table by the time they finished telling them of Pale Daughter's father's death and her sad departure from Apovini. The words of their ancestors echoed in their ears—"Soul on fire"; "Love your wife"; "Teach your daughters"; "We will be together again in this life or the next."

"I can't believe all that she had to go through. Poor Sarah. To see her parents murdered, and her father give her to an Indian, and for that father to have to give her up to a white man his daughter didn't love, and she did it for the love of her people—it sends chills down my spine," Grandma said.

"Apovini really did teach the men of his family how to love. My husband and all his fathers before him are known to be the best husbands. Apovini was also a great chief. They fulfilled each other's wishes. I truly hope their spirits found each other," Belle said.

"I think they did," Anthony said, squeezing Evey's hand under the table.

"Evey," Belle said, grabbing her hand on the table, "you know it's your right to lead our people if you wish. You are the descendent of the first chief."

Evey looked at Anthony and at Belle and said, "I have found a love for our people but didn't have a chance to grow up with them. I trust in Pale Daughter's choice, and Where the Wind Blows should take place of chief, and I will stand by his side and support his every decision."

Anthony and Belle both squeezed her hands hard, and Belle let a few tears fall from her eyes.

"You are wise, granddaughter of my heart, and my grandson is lucky to have your support. I am proud to call you part of our family," Belle said, smiling at her and her grandson.

Evey's grandparents were nodding with approval too. Their granddaughter had made such a responsible, honorable decision. After they talked a while longer, they all retired to bed.

"Come on Tudley. Let's go to bed," Evey said.

But her dog just looked at her and then looked at Anthony.

"Are you trading me in for Anthony?" she asked, abashed.

"I think I just drop more crumbs than you at the table," Anthony said, laughing.

"Well, fine then, you traitor. I'll be in my bed," she said and went to her room.

Evelyn lay in her bed, missing the buffalo painting that she had become accustomed to seeing. Her mind wouldn't shut off from all the day's events. Belle's gift, the brown dream catcher, was hanging up above her bed. But it was going to do her little good if she couldn't even fall asleep. She felt guilty that she was glad Danny messed up so she could be free to love Anthony. But Anthony would be leaving in a few days to go back to the reservation. What then?

She got up. Sleep wasn't going to find her that night.

Evey tried to sneak quietly through the house. She needed to get to her tree so she could just sit and think. She had on sweats. The air would be cold now that the sun was down. She made it to the back door and slowly pulled it open and made her way out. She was quiet, but she wasn't the only one who couldn't sleep.

Anthony saw her sneak out, and he quietly made his way to the kitchen window and watched Evey walk out in the moonlight to her tree, kick off her house slippers, and climb up to her spot. He smiled seeing this. To Anthony, she really was Indian to the bone. He thought about going out to join her but wasn't sure if she just needed a moment to herself, and then he saw her shiver. He could go out and take a blanket to her at least, and if she didn't want him there, he would come back in.

He grabbed a blanket and made his way to the tree. She was looking up at the moon when he got there.

"Evey, I brought a blanket. I saw you shiver. I can give it to you and go back in if you want to be alone," he said, really hoping she wouldn't mind him at least sitting with her.

She looked down at him and smiled.

God, she is beautiful, especially in moonlight, Anthony marveled.

"Climb up and sit with me. I'll be warmer if I have you and a blanket," she said, still smiling.

He smiled back and threw the blanket over his shoulder and climbed up. She scooted over to give him room.

"You shared your spot with me, I can share mine with you," she said, scooting back over to him to get his warmth, and slipped under the blanket.

He smiled at this, thinking of her on his rock.

"Do you think the rock you saw was my rock?" he asked.

She smiled and said, "I know it was."

He took a deep breath. "So it's all true then, isn't it?"

"What's all true?" she asked.

"All the stories passed down of great love and sacrifice and what is to come—two souls on fire reunited in this life."

He put his arms around her, and she lay her head on his shoulder.

"It's true. You said you would set my soul on fire. The truth is, it's been burning since the first time I sat my hand on your face and looked into your eyes. I knew it then, I just was too scared to admit it. Who really falls in love at first sight?" she said.

"We do," he replied and then he picked her chin up to him and kissed her on the mouth.

It was just a soft, simple kiss; and he looked at her. He saw the fire in her eyes, and she felt their hearts beating as one. They kissed again but the type of kiss no one can describe. It was just the imperfect world becoming perfect in such a real, true moment. Their mouths fit perfectly together, and their tongues danced in perfect rhythm to each other. They kissed for a long time, savoring the touch, the taste, the sound, and the feeling. Her heart was beating fast.

He looked at her and told her in their language, "It is my heart that beats for you."

She smiled at him and said, "And mine for you. My soul isn't just on fire—it is roaring."

Then she kissed him again—this time, biting his lip a little. And then they settled into each other's arm and they watched the moon watch them.

Two owls came and landed on the branch next to them, and they looked over at them.

"I found him," Evey said, smiling.

"And I'll love her right," Anthony said, also smiling.

The owls nestled into each other as if cuddling, and both of them smiled. The owls had led her to her people.

"Do you think Apovini and Pale Daughter's spirits are on their wings?" she asked aloud.

"I know they are."

This special moment was being seen from the kitchen window where two grandmothers were crying and holding hands, witnessing the last threads of the spiderweb being woven. The final thread was placed when the owls landed on the branch that Evey and Anthony were sitting on.

Grandma gasped, and Belle said, "Look. It's them."

They watched until the owls finally flew off. It was at least an hour.

Belle nudged Grandma then and said, "We should rest."

But it was really because she felt they imposed on a special moment that their grandchildren were experiencing. Was it wrong she was happy to see them kiss? A grandmother would be upset to see that, but she knew their souls were on fire for each other and that only they could be what the other needed.

When the owls flew off, Anthony and Evey decided to climb down too.

When they got to the ground, she asked, "Will you teach me the Dance of the Wind?"

He looked at her and smiled. "If that's what you want."

She nodded. So he took her hand and sat the blanket on the ground and began to teach her the stomps and jumps and hand movements, and they laughed and whirled together in perfect unison. They danced until they were tired and their faces hurt from smiling. They sat down with a thud in front of the tree, using its massive trunk for support.

"You're a lot of fun, you know that?" Anthony asked her.

"That's good because I sure like laughing with you. I haven't smiled or laughed this much . . . well, since my parents died," she said, thinking back.

He pulled her in close and wrapped the blanket around them.

"I promise to try to always be a reason for you to smile," he said, kissing her forehead.

She sighed and lay into him. She burned for him, and she told him so.

"I don't understand how it's possible to feel the way I do about you after only knowing you for such a short while, but I really do burn for you. How is it even possible?"

He shrugged his shoulders. "Life is a crazy thing, but love is something different all in itself. It's like it has a life of its own within you. I've thought I felt love before—and I did—but this is way different. I feel as if though now that I've admitted it, and we've only but kissed, I can't live without you. You are what I can't live without."

That's all she needed to hear. She kissed him with such passion, it took his breath away. Their hearts were both beating fast and with intent. Their hearts knew their job was to beat and keep beating so that their moment together could live.

"Anthony, I want you to have me," she said.

"Are you sure? We have plenty of time," he said to her, looking at her very intently, pulling her back to him.

She looked him in the eye. "I want you to have me, and I you. I need you now."

That's all he needed to hear. He knew after this step, that would be it. He would forever be hers, and that was okay. He kissed her gently and with purpose. He kissed her hands and put them on his face and looked into her eyes. The moonlight hit them just right, and he swore they sparkled. She saw something flicker in his eyes too. Her soul belonged to him now, and they hadn't even made love yet.

It was chilly out, but she wanted to feel his skin on hers. She lifted his shirt up over his head and took hers off. It was cold, and goose bumps rippled over her whole body. Her light pink nipples stood up, and he looked her over and shuddered. Her beautiful white breasts and to see the goosebumps dance on her skin were almost enough to take him over the top. He lowered his head to kiss them.

She arched her back and put a hand in his hair. She needed him. She reached for his sweatpants and was groping to find what she was looking for. It didn't take long as he was ready. She grasped him hard, and he let his breath out in a gasp on her breast and lifted his head to take her mouth in his. Then he put his hand down her sweatpants to find her ready for him. He slid them down and gently laid her down on the ground with their shirts under her, and he got on top of her and looked into her eyes again.

In their language she said, "Please, please take me. I'm yours, Beat of My Heart."

"And I am yours," Anthony told her, smiling and plunging deep inside her.

It took her breath away. It felt so right, so perfect, as if he was the last piece of the puzzle placed seamlessly where it belonged. He moved inside her, and she spread herself open to him and grabbed his behind to pull him in deeper. He moaned and put his mouth on hers and kissed her hard as he moved faster. She pulled his hair so he would pull up. She wanted to see his face. She wanted to remember her moment of surrender to the flames of her soul.

He looked down at her, as if looking to memorize her too. Unlike their ancestors, this was their beginning, not their ending, and he went in hard and hit her core. She arched her back to meet him, and he grabbed her breasts and shoved in hard again and again, until they were both breathless.

Then he rolled over with her on top him, never coming out of her, and pulled her hips down hard on him, and she moaned. She started to move methodically on him and was thinking how right it was and how he just fit her perfectly. He was made for her.

She sat up on him and took his hands to her breast and looked down at him and smiled, and he returned the smile. She started moving faster, and he closed his eyes, trying to hold on for her. She went even faster, and he was at his breaking point, and she leaned down and put her mouth right next to his ear where he could hear her breathing hard. She rammed upward and then down on him hard, and he let out a moan.

At that moment, she whispered in his ear, "Let's go together."

Anthony's eyes bulged, and he looked at her.

"Now. Oh, Anthony. Now," Evey moaned.

They could have sworn the earth shook. To have that type of ecstasy run through her entire body all but immobilized her. He felt it too. Neither one had ever experienced that. She fell down on top of him, completely exhausted from their efforts.

They were thoroughly enveloped in each other when two owl feathers floated down from the tree. They saw them fall.

Evey rolled off him to grab them.

"I think we've just come full circle. They are together now in this lifetime, because of us," she said stroking the feathers and looking up to see him smiling at her.

"I'm totally okay with my soul on fire for you, if this is what I get for the rest of my life," he said.

"I'm okay with it too, Beat of My Heart," Evey said, smiling back.

They put their clothes back on. It was too cool to be without clothes, if you weren't otherwise engaged.

She giggled.

"What are you laughing at?" Anthony asked.

"I'm just thinking about what happened," she said, her face flushed pink.

"And it makes you laugh? I'm not sure if that's a good thing," he said eyeing her.

"Oh, it is good," she said, leaning in to kiss him.

"How in the world am I supposed to go back to New Mexico with you here?" he asked her.

"I have no idea, but if Apovini and Pale Daughter could wait generations, I think we can handle a few months," she replied.

He kissed her forehead. "I guess, but I'm not going to like it."

They laughed and talked, and the next thing they knew, two grandmothers were outside looking down at them.

"What in the world are you two doing out here still?" Grandma questioned.

"Still?" Anthony asked, feeling groggy.

They must have fallen asleep against the tree.

"Still?" asked Evey.

"We saw you two come out here last night and the owls land in the tree by you," Belle chimed in, smiling. "They are together again."

"And they left us a gift," Evey said, smiling and handing Belle the owl feathers, knowing that she and Anthony now would have these for their hair.

"How long did you watch from the window?" Anthony asked, trying not to sound guilty.

"Just until the owls flew off. Then we both went back to bed," Belle said.

"Yes. I may have looked over my shoulder to see you teaching Evey the wind dance," Grandma said, laughing.

"Well, it does look silly when you do it yourself," Anthony added, laughing.

"How did you sleep out here on the dark ground?" Grandma asked.

"It's the best sleep I've ever gotten. I feel safe with Anthony, and dreams don't haunt me when he's with me," Evey said.

Belle nodded her approval.

"All right, inside for breakfast, the two of you," Grandma said.

Evey and Anthony got up to follow them.

Belle said over her shoulder, "We still haven't opened the pot either."

Evey already knew what was in there though, so she felt no rush.

"In good time," she said.

"How did you sleep, Belle?" Grandma was asking her.

"Oh, very well. I was tired," she replied.

"I slept pretty well myself but had the craziest dream. I dreamt of an earthquake," Grandma said.

Evey looked at Anthony who was smiling to himself.

"I thought I felt the earth shake beneath us," she whispered to him.

Anthony squeezed her hand.

Belle turned around and said, "What is it, Daughter?"

"Oh, nothing. I'm starving," Evey quickly said, smiling.

Belle eyed her and said, "I bet so after a night outdoors."

They forget things travel to her on the wind. She gave a little smile, but who was she to stand in the way of love? They've only just found one another and have a lifetime to go and many things to still find out.

Who would have thought the black gumbo would bring a daughter home with an arrowhead?